Dedication

I dedicate this to Mom, Dad, Peggy, and Barbara. You taught me what a loving family should be and always made sure I knew where I belonged. I love you!

Nadavir Kids Club

Deb has created a set of FREE activities for kids aged 8-12 years to enjoy when you join the Nadavir Kids Club! There are games, puzzles, crafts, stories and other fun activities in the Clubhouse.

Parents, grandparents, guardians, aunts, uncles, and educators will receive a FREE newsletter with a new activity every month and updates on Deb's books and events to share with the children and students in their lives.

Sign up here: https://www.debcushman.com

Please Leave a Review!

Reviews are extremely important for letting others know about *Ping's Mystery in Pixiandria!* When you have finished reading this book, please leave a review at the book vendor you use or where you purchased the book. Thank you!

Contents

CHAPTER 1

Seeing Things

Ping's faery senses tingled. She glimpsed someone flitting above her as she soared through the tunnels of Nadavir on the way to defense class. Flickering glowworm lanterns cast a soft, golden light on the rough stone walls, but didn't reveal any hidden observers.

This curious sensation of being watched had plagued her all week. As the tiny faery flew, she'd spot something, like an eyelash clinging stubbornly to the edge of her sight. But it wasn't an eyelash, a speck of dirt, or a piece of lint. Nothing was there. The more it happened, the more her curiosity grew, and so did her frustration.

Realizing her hair had probably turned purple from annoyance at the mysterious illusion, she switched it to a confident blue, which matched her dress and camouflaged her in the ceiling's shadows.

As she skillfully maneuvered through the familiar mountain dwarf colony, her butterfly wings fluttered soundlessly. Each movement was deliberate, guided by the words in her head: cautious, observant, furtive, silent. This was practice and preparation. What was she training for? She wasn't sure, but being small and vulnerable made speed and cleverness her main powers against an enemy. When the trolls had held the Nadavir menfolk captive last year, that quick cunning had proven important to Ping in helping the colony's females defeat those nasty villains.

"Shivering sandstone!" Frigg's voice echoed from below. "What are you doing?" Ping's loyal dwarf friend hurried toward the vast cavern ahead. "We'll be late!"

"I saw it again," Ping called down, her voice urgent. "Something's here, just beyond my grasp."

Frigg sighed, her impatience clear. She glanced up. "I don't see anything."

"You never do," Ping replied. "Maybe you need your eyes checked."

Shaking her head, Frigg sped up. Together, they reached the cavern's entrance, slipping through just before their weaponry teacher, Dagny, shut the door with a stern frown.

Tapestries adorned the walls of the practice hall, depicting legendary battles and heroic dwarf deeds. In the center, a grand stone platform stood, serving as the stage for Dagny's demonstrations. Its intricate carvings depicted ancient runes and symbols of protection.

"Gather 'round!" Dagny's voice rang out. The girls

eagerly awaited the announcement of the day's defense skill—a secret yet to be unveiled, much like the elusive presence that haunted Ping's every flutter.

Ping landed on Frigg's shoulder and whispered, knowing her breath tickled her friend's ear. "I tell you, something's there, something small—an insect, perhaps. It's messing with me."

Frigg muttered. "Why would an insect want to bug you?"

"I don't know, but I've seen it out of the corner of my eye several times now."

Frigg's shrug nearly dislodged Ping, threatening to send her spiraling. They joined the other female students clustered against the wall. Among the dwarves stood other magical girls as well: brownies, gnomes, elves, and even goblins.

Dagny called for their attention. "Today, we'll practice brandishing our weapons and jabbing at our opponents."

"What does brandishing mean?" Ping asked.

Dagny demonstrated with a wooden practice sword. "You will display your weapon and wave it with a flourish. Then you will jab it forward. Wave and jab."

"Here, Ping," Dagny waved a straight pin, its silver glint catching the light. "This pin shall be your sword."

"Brilliant!" Ping said with a laugh.

"You're small as a hummingbird," Dagney continued. "It darts among the flowers. I want you to picture a hummingbird and think, up, down, zig, zag. That's the way you'll evade your enemies. Wave and jab as a last resort."

Frigg giggled. "That pin's sharp. Hope she doesn't jab herself."

Ping gave her a frosty glare and snatched the pin from Dagny's fingers. She waggled it in front of Frigg's nose and shouted, "Wave and jab!"

Frigg covered her eyes and ducked out of poking range

"Ladies," Dagny clapped her hands, her gaze serious. "What's the first rule of weaponry?"

In perfect harmony, everyone recited, "Safety first!"

As the girls practiced their skills, their laughter and chatter filled the cavern, creating a lively atmosphere.

Ping flew off to try out her new pin sword on a practice dummy, a bag of sand attached to a pole. As she turned, she caught movement flickering out of reach. She raced to where she'd seen it, but the space was empty.

She sighed and pictured a worthy foe about to attack her. *Up, down, zig, zag.* Then she shook the pin and waved it in a jabbing motion. *Wave and jab.* She smoothed the rhythm as she thought about how she'd carry the pin with her without piercing herself. What could she use as a sheath? The answer was as elusive as the unseen observer.

When she tired, Ping sat on a wall sconce and patted the head of the glowworm snuggled inside, his light a beacon in the cave's dark shadows. She watched her fellow trainees practice their skills. Their progress had been remarkable since their clumsy, yet triumphant battle against the trolls who had attacked the colony.

She remembered that fateful clash when the female

what might be true. But some new questions arose: Were Sycamore and Zinnia going to marry? Was life better under King Rowan's reign? Were the humans plotting to invade Pixiandria?

Yet, she'd gained no clues to her mother's whereabouts. She hoped the answer would come, carried on the wings of her new friends or revealed in palace whispers to Chia's spies.

CHAPTER 19

Answers and Magic

Violetta entered Ping's chamber, eyes widening at the sight before her. Crumbs scattered like confetti on the floor. She plucked a feather from the air and giggled. "What happened in here?"

Ping replied with a playful twinkle in her eye. "A few special visitors fluttered by."

"Really? I didn't see anyone enter or leave your chamber."

"Yes, well, you wouldn't have," Ping said mysteriously. "If you'll help me dress, I'd like to see The Ancient One this morning. Do we need to send word?"

"Probably, just to make sure she's home. But you are the Princess, and you can go anywhere you like."

"Let's do the polite thing and ask her. I'll get dressed while we await her answer. I wouldn't want to upset her."

Violetta left to send the message while Ping chose a dazzling red gown with silver ruffles that shimmered in the light and released the scent of roses. She rushed to dress, but the oodles of buttons proved a challenge. Violetta's nimble fingers completed the task when she returned.

When a messenger announced that The Ancient One would love to see the Princess, they navigated the twisty passages to the wise woman's chamber. The Ancient One greeted Ping with open arms. She offered tea, fruit, and a sly wink. "I thought you might enjoy something other than pastries. You probably had your fill this morning with your winged friends."

"How did you know?" Ping's surprise blended with a touch of annoyance that everyone seemed to know her business.

"You'll find I know a great deal."

"I guess that's good, because I came to learn more about my mother."

"I know that your mother loves you very much. It's why she sent you away, to keep you from the storm of courtly strife and to keep you safe from the darkness that claimed your father."

"I don't understand."

"Following King Rowan's mysterious death, conflict broke out between various factions at court. Many blamed your mother and threatened her. She worried about you and sent you away."

"Why was my father's death mysterious?" Ping asked.

"He was healthy one day, but the next, he fell ill

and died, leaving behind many unanswered questions. Some suspected poison, but the healers couldn't say for sure, and they found no proof."

"Wasn't my mother worried about herself?"

"Her powerful magic was her shield."

"But she's disappeared."

"Yes," The Ancient One confirmed. "She vanished, leaving behind an even bigger mystery."

"With so many people around, how could she just disappear?" Ping asked, her voice laced with hope and fear.

"That is the question we all ask. It's as though she has become a light breeze, felt but unseen."

"Felt?" Ping echoed, her mind racing with questions.

The Ancient One's gaze was steady. "Some relationships run deeper than sight, sensed in our heart and soul. When I focus on a faery, my magic weaves a connection, allowing me to sense their presence and their feelings."

"Can you feel what she's thinking?"

"Unfortunately, my magic isn't so precise. But I can often tell if they are touched by joy, shadowed by sorrow, or gripped by fear. I have weakly sensed Queen Aster's life force, so I'm sure she's alive, but her emotions have been silent to me since she disappeared."

"Can pixies shift their shapes or become invisible?" Ping asked, contemplating Frigg's shapeshifting and the trolls' ability to camouflage.

The Ancient One regarded Ping thoughtfully before replying. "Invisibility is not within our powers, but yes, most pixies can shape shift. But only into insects, usually their aspect insect."

Ping sat up, her curiosity piqued. "Aspect insect?"

The Ancient One unfurled her wings, pale green, almost translucent with long, curving tails that trailed from the bottoms. Her wings also sported two spots, resembling eyes. She transformed into a beautiful insect with the same wing pattern.

"A butterfly?" Ping asked.

"A moth," The Ancient One replied, "specifically, a Luna Moth, sometimes called a Moon Moth."

"I guess since I didn't grow up around other pixies, I didn't realize our wings were so different!"

The Ancient One nodded. "Yes, you'd have learned from an early age that each pixie's wings reflect their aspect insect. Your butterfly wings grant you the ability to transform into one. It is said our spirits were once insects, and this bond forms the essence of our being."

"Butterfly!" The idea of shifting into a butterfly thrilled Ping, and she shivered with excitement. So much to take in! Suddenly, she knew what Frigg must have felt that first time she accidentally shifted into a rock, and they'd had to figure out how she could change back!

"Can we explore this shifting magic tomorrow? I need time to think."

The Ancient One assured her with a compassionate smile. "Yes, my dear, we shall delve into transformation's mysteries when you are ready."

Ping remembered her purpose in coming. "Lord Sycamore and Aunt Iris have both said they want me to act as queen until my mother returns."

"What are your thoughts about that?"

"I'm not sure," Ping confessed. "I put on a decent act at the Kaboodle meeting. But I didn't feel in charge, and I think they hate me."

"While it's possible you unsettled things, I don't believe they hold any malice toward you. Having no leadership is scary for Pixiandria."

"Zinnia seemed to handle things. I think she wants to rule."

"Yes, she's very good at telling people what to do."

"Why did she send Lord Sycamore to find me? Why didn't she just take over?"

The Ancient One considered. "Perhaps she seeks to guide you. On the other hand, she might want to show that she would be the better queen by contrasting your lively nature with her wisdom."

"She doesn't know me very well. I may be fanciful sometimes, but I'm capable of serious ideas."

"Whatever her goal, her power is immense. Be careful," The Ancient One cautioned.

"My deepest desire is to find my mother and restore her to the throne," Ping said. "Then I can go home to Nadavir."

The Ancient One studied her, a question in her gaze. "Are you so sure Nadavir is where you belong?"

Ping felt like a butterfly caught in a strong wind. "Everything is so strange here. I don't feel comfortable. Nadavir is my cocoon," she sighed, "where everything is cozy and familiar."

"Ah, yes, little butterfly. But sometimes you must flutter beyond your comfortable cocoon. It is how you discover new flowers and learn to soar."

Ping's heart longed for her friends—Frigg's laughter, Birgit's hugs, Dvalin's gruffness, Tip's playful antics, and Cricall's steadfast presence.

"They genuinely care about me in Nadavir. It feels like everyone here wants to hold back my wings so I can't fly."

"I care about you," The Ancient One said, her voice as warm as the sun. "I see your wings are ready to spread, and soon, others will see it too.

"They want to stare and gawk. Except for Thorn and Violetta, I've made more loyal friends among the birds and bees."

"Let's weave some magic together," The Ancient One suggested. "You have magic as vibrant as the sun, waiting to be channeled." She tapped her chin. "Were you able to practice yesterday?"

"I called a bird to me," Ping said, her face alight with wonder. "It heard my silent wish and flew through my window as if answering a royal summons."

"That's a promising start!" The Ancient One exclaimed. "Did it fly out again?"

"Eventually. After we exchanged stories."

"You spoke with it?" Her eyebrow arched like a curious caterpillar.

"And butterflies and bees as well. They all returned today, much to Violetta's dismay at the mess."

"What an amazing gift you have!"

"Gift?"

"A rare gift. To speak with birds and butterflies is a magic not known to all pixies," she said.

"In Nadavir, even the smallest mouse has a voice. When the trolls threatened our lives, every creature rallied to our side, from a tiny ant to a giant salamander," Ping recounted with pride.

The Ancient One's gaze filled with wonder. "I've never heard such a thing."

"We have messenger mice who scurry through Nadavir with notes, keeping everyone connected. How do pixies share messages?"

"Well, some pixies have telepathic abilities and can speak to others in their minds."

Ping's face brightened. "Like Violetta! I can call her by shouting in my mind."

The Ancient One's chiming laugh filled the air. "Yes, something like that. But most simply speak face-to-face."

"Why can I speak with creatures when others can't?" Ping asked.

The Ancient One thought for a long time before answering. "I believe your magic blossomed in Nadavir, manifesting itself for your survival. Everyone in Nadavir speaks to the creatures, so your magic developed that ability in you."

Ping grinned. "It's nice to know I can befriend a spider if I want."

"It certainly makes you unique!" The Ancient One said. "I'm eager to see what magic will awaken in you here in Pixiandria."

"I'd never considered magic to be alive."

"Let's see what you can do. Close your eyes and focus on an object. Perhaps something inside the palace this time."

Ping closed her eyes. An object. What object has she seen that she could focus on? Her mother's portrait hanging in the Kaboodle chamber popped into her mind.

"Do you have something?"

"Yes, it's..."

"Don't tell me. Let that image fill your thoughts," The Ancient One encouraged, her voice soft. "Imagine it rising, floating like a leaf caught in a gentle breeze, then return it to its original spot. Relax your tension."

Ping's face, once scrunched in concentration, relaxed as she imagined the painting drifting to the ceiling and returning to its place on the wall. "It worked!"

"Beautifully done! Open your eyes and select an object in this room. You'll make it rise, not only in your mind, but in the physical world."

Ping's gaze landed on a teacup, but The Ancient One said, "Let's start with something that won't shatter. How about a pillow?"

Ping chose a lovely red pillow as dazzling as her dress. With a thought, the pillow lifted, floating across the room, and then settled back into the chair.

The Ancient One watched, her eyes reflecting a decision she'd made. "You're ready," she declared with a nod.

"Ready for what?" Ping asked.

With a smile and a flick of her wrist, The Ancient One produced a golden wand, its end adorned with a shimmering star. "Ready for your wand. You've tamed your magic, and now it's time to amplify it."

"Wow!" Ping cried, her eyes wide with wonder. "A wand! What do I do with it?"

"Your natural magical abilities strengthen with a wand." She handed it to Ping, who accepted it gingerly. "Focus on the pillow again, eyes open, and flick the wand lightly."

As Ping concentrated on the pillow, she could feel the energy of her magic tingling in the air. She flicked her wand, and the pillow zoomed to the ceiling.

"Whoa!" Ping cried. "This will take some getting used to!"

The Ancient One laughed. "Yes, practice will harness your energy, and it will make you a truly powerful faery. Now, guide the pillow by pointing your wand."

Ping did as instructed. The pillow floated down.

The door burst open with a bang, and Violetta rushed in, her face flushed. "Forgive me for interrupting, but we have a crisis! Lady Zinnia has disappeared!"

CHAPTER 20

What Happened to Zinnia?

The palace was abuzz with worry. A whirlwind of wings and urgent voices filled the halls. Ping hovered amidst the hustle. The word chaos seemed too tame to describe the scene. First the Queen and now Lady Zinnia had vanished without a trace.

As they flew through the halls, Violetta told Ping that Zinnia's attendants had found her chamber empty this morning and assumed she was taking her customary glide through the palace gardens. As the sun climbed higher and she hadn't returned, worry blossomed. They alerted the guard, but a search produced no trace of her. With the Queen also missing, fears of a sinister pattern surfaced.

Ping wanted to speak to Lord Sycamore. When she spotted Thorn in a corridor, she called to him. "Do you know where your father is?"

"I haven't seen him since Dawn Delicacies. He's

likely in the Kaboodle chamber, planning the search for Lady Zinnia."

"Would you guide me there? The palace corridors are like a labyrinth, twisting and turning in a never-ending maze of confusion."

"With pleasure, Ping."

Ping turned to Violetta. "Please see what you can find out." Violetta rushed away.

Thorn and Ping maneuvered through the crowds who cluttered the corridors, gossiping about Zinnia's disappearance. Thorn, swift and sure, announced her royal status and cleared a path for Ping through the startled pixies. Hand in hand, they reached the meeting room's doors.

Thorn didn't hesitate. He pushed the door open. Inside, more chaos reigned, with everyone shouting over one another until Lord Sycamore's piercing whistle commanded silence.

Ping rushed to his side. "Thank you for gathering everyone so quickly, Lord Sycamore. Is there any news?"

Lord Sycamore's features softened from frustration to reassurance. "Our forces scoured the land, yet Lady Zinnia's fate remains elusive."

Ping's heart sank, her worry clear in her voice. "That is distressing. How can I help?"

He cleared his throat. "Your willingness to help is generous, but your unfamiliarity with the palace and realm limits your role. You could reassure your subjects. If they see you among them, displaying calm, they will be comforted."

She could see his point. Though she probably should be in control, Ping was clueless about how to proceed. She knew little about Zinnia, the palace, or the kingdom. If she tried to organize the search, she'd only get in the way.

Ping cast a quick glance at Thorn. "You are right. If Thorn lends a hand, I'll join my subjects in the palace corridors and garden paths to comfort them."

"Yes, Princess. An excellent suggestion. We'll keep you informed." He turned back to Lord Evergreen and their search plans.

Throughout the day, Thorn led Ping through the various gatherings of pixies. She frequently paused and introduced herself to a group, asking them questions about their families and sharing hopeful words about the search for Lady Zinnia. The bustling and chaotic chats of the palace hallways were a stark contrast to the peaceful and serene conversations in the gardens. Many pixies rushed to meet her and talk about Lady Zinnia's disappearance.

When she returned to her chamber, Violetta awaited her with tea and peach tarts. Ping shared her day's activities. "I should have been out speaking to everyone long before Zinnia disappeared. They were eager to talk with me."

"Oh, yes, they are curious about their princess. You've lived quite a different life from pixies in Pixiandria, and they want to hear about your experiences."

That evening, snuggled into her bed, those friendly wishes she'd received from the pixies brought contentment. She could finally envision herself belonging to Pixiandria, a once impossible goal now within reach.

A noise in the corner made her snap her fingers, and a warm glow brightened the room. She watched with eager eyes as Chia, the mouse spy, skittered from the gap in the baseboard.

"Chia, you've returned!" she cried. "I'm so happy to see your whiskered face again!"

The mouse removed his walnut shell hat and dipped his head in a tiny bow. "Yes, Missy Ping, I'm cheery, cheery, cherry to see you, and I have oodles to report."

"Do tell," Ping urged, leaning forward.

"The mean lady has disappeared."

"The mean lady?"

"Yes, mean, mean, mean to crawling creatures, especially spiders. She's known for her stomps and squashes." Chia sniffled. "I have lost so many dear friends to her ruthless foot and hand."

"I'm sorry to hear that, Chia." Ping's heart ached for the little mouse's loss.

"Yes, it's so, so, so sad. And now, she's vanished."

"Have any of your friends seen where she went?"

Chia's ears twitched. "No one saw her leave. We don't like her, but I knew you'd want to know what happened to her. I've rallied my critters to search high and low from towers to dungeons."

Ping's eyes widened. "Dungeons? There are dungeons?"

"Indeed, Missy Ping, deep, dark, dank dungeons."

Ping hesitated. "Do we put anyone in the dungeons?"

"Not so much now," Chia reassured her. "I guess they used to in the way-back days."

Ping made a mental note to ask Lord Sycamore what happened to people who broke the law in Pixiandria. Nadavir had a jail, but it was seldom used.

"I'm glad your team is on the lookout. Any other hidden places she might be?"

Chia shivered, his voice dropping to a hush. "Only the Dark Lands."

"Where are they?"

"Nobody knows. But it's said that a portal in the dungeons leads to the Dark Lands," Chia murmured. "It's a place of legend. Stories that would scare the tail right off you. Even the bravest fear it."

"A portal in the dungeons?" Ping asked, her thoughts racing. "That sounds alarming."

"If there's a portal, it's well, well, well hidden."

A spark of determination flared within Ping. "Then I must learn more about this portal and the Dark Lands. It could be the clue we need to find my mother and Lady Zinnia."

"Missy Ping, no, no, no! Too dangerous. You must not go there!"

Ping offered a comforting pat to Chia's head. "I never said I'd go to the Dark Lands. But I need to know more. If you can discover anything, it'd be helpful."

Chia nodded, though his tiny eyes still showed a flicker of fear. His voice dropped to a hush. "I'll try, try, try, but even mentioning that place sends shivers through cautious critters."

"I'll check with The Ancient One tomorrow to

see what she knows." Ping tapped her chin, deep in thought. "If there's a chance my mother or Lady Zinnia might be there, I must explore every lead."

Chia trembled. "Please, please, please be careful."

"I will, and you be careful, too. I don't want you or any of your friends getting stomped on."

"We are sneaky and stay away from the enormous feet and hands of pixies." His squeaky voice hinted at pride.

Ping bit back a chuckle. Pixies? Big feet and hands? The very idea! But she had experience being the smallest one in the room and didn't want to insult her tiny friend, so she buried her amusement deep inside.

The following day's Dawn Delicacies in the grand hall was a somber event infused with mournful consumption of berry tarts and acorn biscuits. An uncertainty filled the room in the absence of the Queen and Lady Zinnia. Ping had run out of comforting words for the sorrowful pixies. She escaped as quickly as she could to visit The Ancient One.

The time spent in the palace hallways yesterday had made the passages less mysterious. They greeted her like old friends, and the tapestries seemed to sway in recognition of her achievement in finding her own way.

"I hope you don't mind my unannounced visit," Ping said, after The Ancient One had welcomed her.

With a sparkle in her wise old eyes, The Ancient One replied, "My dear Princess, your presence is a joy at any hour."

"Thank you. I appreciate that."

"What stirs you from your royal chamber today? Is it a quest for knowledge, or perhaps a craving for my special blend of pine needle tea?" The Ancient One teased.

Ping laughed. "Your tea is delicious, but I also need information about the Dark Lands."

The Ancient One raised an eyebrow. "How did such tales reach your ears?"

"Oh, people talk."

"But the Dark Lands? Not your typical topic for idle chit-chat."

Ping tried to sound casual as she said, "I've heard rumors about a portal to the Dark Lands in the palace dungeons. Did you know there were dungeons beneath our feet?"

The Ancient One fixed a thoughtful gaze on Ping. "I was aware. They are relics of a bygone era, untouched and unused."

Ping wrinkled her nose. "They must be bleak. I can't imagine what you'd have to do to be sentenced to a cell in a dark dungeon." She shuddered. "And the portal?"

"Yes, I've heard rumors. If true, its location and purpose remain a secret."

Ping leaned forward. "Who would have more information about this mystery?"

"Your mother might know more." Her gaze drifted to her towering bookshelves. "My books do not share that knowledge, but maybe the truth lies within the pages of a volume in the palace tree library."

Ping remembered Lord Sycamore pulling a book

from the palace library column as they ascended the steps to her chamber that first night.

Her thoughts were interrupted by The Ancient One's voice. "The Dark Lands are a legend kept alive by rumors. Why this sudden interest?"

"I'm curious to learn everything I can about Pixiandria." Ping's curiosity was a flame that couldn't be quenched. "What do rumors say about the Dark Lands? I'm already guessing they're dark."

"The stories talk of a realm where shadows reign, creatures of nightmares roam free, and the air is heavy with the scent of despair," The Ancient One explained, her voice laced with caution. "They are dreadful tales of evils that would curl your wings!"

Ping gulped. "Such a place seems better left in the storybook realm."

"Indeed, it does," The Ancient One agreed. She took a sip of her tea. "Some stories are best left untold, and some lands best left unexplored."

Ping thanked The Ancient One. Then she spread her delicate wings, soaring from the room.

She'd search for Thorn. He'd know how to locate books in the palace library. They held the promise of answers that she desperately sought.

CHAPTER 21

Pluck a Book from the Library

Back in her chamber, Ping practiced calling her wand to her. "Focus on your wand and it will appear in your hand," The Ancient One had said. "When you don't need it, send it away."

Ping summoned the wand with a thought and felt the stick's smooth surface in her hand as though sculpted there.

"Where can I find Thorn?" she asked. The wand tugged her toward the window, where she spotted him in the field with a band of boys, their wings beating enthusiastically as they chased after a zig-zagging object.

She zoomed out the door, down to the gardens, and along a winding path. It didn't take her long to reach the field where she'd seen the boys. One spotted her and said something to the others. They stopped and stared. The object bopped one on the head.

"Princess Ping!" Thorn's voice carried across the

field. He darted toward her, wings tipping in deference. "How can we help you?"

Ping laughed and scanned the group. "First, I'd love to meet your companions, then I have a request."

"Certainly. I'd like to present Birch, Catalpa, Aspen, and Willow." Each boy tipped a wing to her as he bowed. Then they popped up with huge grins.

Ping struggled to keep them straight, but she knew the leaves tangled in their hair would help her distinguish them.

Birch, with his bark-like freckles. displayed small, yellow-green leaves in his hair.

Catalpa's large green eyes matched the huge, heart-shaped leaf perched like a hat on top of his head. Several long, slender seed pods dangled from the leaf.

Aspen's hair sported so many orange-and-yellow leaves he resembled a pumpkin.

And Willow's long ropes of silver-tinged leaves draped stylishly over his shoulders.

"It's wonderful to meet you. I remember Aspen from our chat in the palace hall yesterday."

Aspen blushed and tipped his wing again. "Yes, Your Majesty. I was with my mother and my sister, Rose. She was crying, and you made her feel better. Thank you for your kind words."

Ping frowned and tried to look stern. "Enough formalities. From now on, call me Ping. It's not royal protocol, but I'm sure you'll want me to feel comfortable."

Aspen stumbled over his words. "Yes, Your... I mean, Ping."

The others nodded in agreement, their leaves rustling.

Ping giggled. "Let's practice. On the count of three, shout it—PING! That's a royal order."

She counted and, like a tornado, the boys roared, "PING!"

"That's terrific! As you can see, my wings are like those of a butterfly. I'm not familiar with your wing styles. Do you mind my asking what they are?"

Aspen said, "Mine are brown moth wings."

"Bumblebee for me," said Birch. His were orangish brown.

Catalpa turned proudly, so she could see that his wings were red dragonfly.

Willow shyly showed her his whitefly wings.

Thorn displayed his orange-and-white moth wings. "They have a fancy name: Cyana Conclusa. I have no idea what it means!"

"Thank you all for sharing! I have a lot to learn about being a pixie, and I've enjoyed meeting you. Now, back to your game while I borrow Thorn."

Thorn asked, curious, "What might I do for you?"

"I need help to find something in the library."

"I can do that!"

Together, they soared into the palace and flew to the stairs around the wooden column housing the palace library, with its towering bookshelves that felt like a sanctuary for knowledge.

"What information do you seek?" Thorn asked.

"The Dark Lands." When she saw Thorn's eyes widen with surprise, she added, "I know they are dangerous, and people don't talk about them. But this is important."

Thorn swallowed. "Well, to search the library when you don't know a title, you ask the tree to give you any books on the subject."

"Just ask? It's that simple?"

"Yes, he said. "Library, show me books containing information about the Dark Lands."

He flew backward so he could survey the entire library and waited. The column's tree-like bark seemed to ripple, awakening and searching. "Follow me," Thorn circled, up and down, scanning each crevice.

"What's wrong?" Ping asked.

"It's peculiar," Thorn confessed. "The library should nudge out any relevant books, but nothing stirs. Perhaps you should try. Maybe it reserves such knowledge for royalty."

Ping produced her wand for an extra boost. She took a deep breath and echoed Thorn's words.

They circled the tree, searching for a response, but again, silence greeted them.

"I guess it doesn't have the information you seek," Thorn said.

Ping sighed. "Thanks for the lesson. Please enjoy the afternoon with your friends."

As Thorn flew away, Ping gazed at the ancient library. Where else might she seek answers?

When Ping fluttered into the grand hall for Moonlight Morsels that night, the courtiers remained somber. The aroma of freshly baked berry cakes and acorn biscuits wafted through the room, mingling with the courtiers' hushed tones that silenced as she made her way to the head table.

Lord Sycamore was nowhere to be seen. She wondered where he could be and hoped he wasn't missing, too. Their meals were usually a delightful affair, packed with laughter and tales of his youth in Pixiandria. But tonight's dinner passed quietly, his absence leaving a void no meal could fill.

As Ping was about to indulge in her dessert, a scrumptious pear pudding cake crowned with fluffy cream topping, Lord Sycamore burst through the double doors.

He glanced around the hall, smiling and greeting everyone as he wove his charisma through the crowd like a silver thread. Even in such solemn times, he lifted pixies' spirits. Ping found her fondness for him growing, a stark contrast to the day he'd whisked her away from Naduvir.

When he reached the head table, he dipped his head in a deep bow and tipped his wing. "Your Majesty, you face shines brighter than the stars tonight."

Ping's cheeks warmed with a blush. "Thank you. You look quite handsome yourself."

A smile quirked his mouth as he took his seat. "What adventures occupied your day, Princess?"

She recounted her day and finished with, "Is there any news about Lady Zinnia?"

Lord Sycamore shook his head, his frown deepening. "No, I chased a few leads and possible sightings, but they led nowhere. The search continues."

Ping wrinkled her brow. "It's so strange, isn't it? For them to vanish without a trace."

"It's a mystery how they could slip away unnoticed."

Thorn entered the hall. He waved to Ping and flew to join them.

Ping said, "Maybe they're lost someplace in the palace."

Lord Sycamore stared. "I can't imagine that Lady Zinnia or Queen Aster would become lost in a palace where they grew up."

Ping leaned in, her voice dropping to a whisper. "I overheard talk of a portal in the dungeons that's said to lead to the Dark Lands. Maybe they found that portal?"

"Dungeons?" Thorn asked, taking his seat on a green cushion.

Lord Sycamore's lips pursed, ignoring his son. "The Dark Lands are mere legend."

"But what if Lady Zinnia and my mother are trapped there?" Ping said, her tone urgent.

Lord Sycamore dismissed the idea with a toss of his hand. "Unlikely. Nobody has used those dungeons in centuries. Even if the Dark Lands exist, why would a portal be located there?"

Ping asked, "Well, it's out of the way. Who would see you going through the portal? Have the dungeons been searched?"

The question caught him off guard and he stammered, "I-I'm sure they have."

Thorn asked, "Would they even think to search the dungeons if they are empty?"

"I've never seen dungeons." Ping paused and pretended to be thinking. "We don't have such things in Nadavir. Oh, we have mines in the lower caverns, but no dungeons."

"Humph," was Sycamore's reply.

She batted her eyelashes. "I'd love a tour. Would you take me to see them?"

Lord Sycamore recoiled. "The dungeons? They're gloomy—no place for a princess."

"I grew up within a mountain. I'm used to dark caves. But you have magic to light things here, so the dungeons couldn't be that dark, even without glow-worms."

"Glowworms?" Thorn asked.

Ping giggled. "Oh, yes, in Nadavir, glowworms light our lanterns! Our glowworm friends beam with joy when tickled, and a gentle pat on their head dims the light to a cozy glow."

"How amazing!" Thorn cried.

Lord Sycamore frowned. "Fascinating as the dungeons may seem, it would not be proper for me to take you there."

Thorn jumped. "I'll take you!" He turned to his father. "A princess must know her realm, from the highest tower to the deepest dungeon."

Her determination clear, Ping said. "Observing every area of the palace is an important part of my education."

Sycamore arched an eyebrow, a wry twist to his lips. "Shall we next visit the sewers?"

Ping ignored him. "Thorn, thank you for offering to take me. Let's go tomorrow." She took another bite of her dessert, the sweetness a contrast to the sour look Lord Sycamore cast toward his son.

"Princess, please be reasonable," Sycamore urged.

Ping pointed to her closed mouth and chewed.

Lord Sycamore sighed and returned to his meal.

Later that night, Chia returned to Ping's room. He had little information to share, other than he'd talked to several of his spies who had searched for the portal. "A promising wall stands at the corridor's end that could hold a portal. But we'd have to know how to open it. Spiders are watching for any action."

The mention of a portal wall in the dungeons fueled Ping's determination to uncover the truth. Pixiandria was thoroughly searched, and the Queen hadn't been found. Maybe she was in the Dark Lands.

That night Ping dreamed she flew into a giant void. The darkness and mist obscured her vision completely. Despite flying for hours, she never reached the other end.

She woke the next morning in a cold sweat, panting and shaking. Doubts swirled like the dark clouds in her dream. Had her mother and Zinnia gone through the portal?

But maybe someone was aware of the portal and what lay beyond. What if her mother was there and needed rescuing? Would Ping have the nerve to go through an unknown portal? And if she did, how would she bring her mother back?

This was a foolish quest. Yet in Nadavir, Frigg had been told that searching for Anasgar was foolish, but it turned out to be the key to defeating the trolls.

CHAPTER 22

The Dungeons

A s the first rays of sun filtered into Ping's chamber, casting a warm glow on the ornate furniture and delicate tapestries, she bounded out of bed.

Violetta's surprise at her mistress's early rising turned to alarm when she heard its purpose. "Oh, Princess, please don't go to such a dreary place. The dungeons will be dark, depressing, and dirty."

"Yes, dungeons are probably all of those things. Would you be my brave companion? We'll need thick cloaks against the cold."

Violetta's eyes grew round as the moon. "Just us?"

"Thorn will guide us," Ping reassured her with a smile.

Violetta's voice quavered. "Thorn?"

"Yes, the three of us. Lord Sycamore was busy."

"Why such a hurry? Why not wait until Lord Sycamore is unbusy? He's better protection than Master Hawthorn."

"Protection from what? An empty dungeon?" Ping sighed. She was tired of arguing about this. Wasn't she a princess? Weren't they supposed to do what she said? "I'm going as soon as I'm ready. I hope you will join me."

Violetta nodded, her loyalty evidently overcoming her worry. "Oh, Princess. I wouldn't let you go without me at your side." She rushed from the chamber.

Ping rummaged through her vast wardrobe for warm clothes. Among the frilly dresses, she found some sparkly pink trousers, a long-sleeved purple blouse, and a stunning navy cloak.

As she finished dressing, there came a knock at the door. Expecting Thorn, Ping called, "Come in."

It was Thorn, but he had his father with him.

"I didn't expect to see you, Lord Sycamore."

"I can't have you wandering the dungeons defenseless, Princess. Who knows what perils lie in wait?"

Thorn's face fell at his father's comment. "I could have protected the Princess!"

Ping smiled. "I would have been incredibly secure with you by my side, Thorn, but now I have the added advantage of defense on both sides! Lord Sycamore, your presence is a welcome surprise. Violetta's joining us in a moment."

Lord Sycamore turned to Ping. "Are you sure I can't talk you out of this? Perhaps you'd like to explore another area of the palace. The greenhouses? The ravens' keep?"

"No, maybe another time. The dungeons will be fine, especially since there aren't any prisoners." She paused. "There aren't any prisoners, are there?"

"No, Your Majesty. They are quite empty."

When Violetta poked her head in the door, Ping said, "Lord Sycamore, would you lead the way?"

The dungeons were indeed as dark, gloomy, and empty as everyone had predicted. There were rows of cells with dirt floors and iron bars. The air was heavy and musty, stuffed with an oppressive sense of despair that seemed to seep into their bones.

Lord Sycamore snapped his fingers, and light orbs appeared. He warned them to stay well away from the iron bars. "Iron is painful to faeries, and they keep faery prisoners near the wall."

"How cruel," Violetta exclaimed.

Thorn agreed. "Such pain and misery."

"Don't feel sorry for them. They earned their agony for their crimes," Sycamore said. "Some say Pixiandria would be better off if we brought back extreme punishments."

Ping asked, "Do you say that?"

"Not most of the time. However, there are moments when I think it might be appropriate."

Ping let the subject drop when she spotted a doorway at the end of the hall. Her curiosity brought her to the top step of a staircase going down. "Where does this lead?"

Thorn was quick to answer. "Must be to the depths below."

Violetta trembled. "You can't want to go any deeper. Who knows what is down there?"

Ping said, "Adventure awaits, and possibly a portal."

Lord Sycamore frowned. "Actually, disappointment awaits. You'll find more empty cells. The portal to the Dark Lands is but a myth."

Ping smiled slyly at him. "Then you won't mind my seeing for myself."

She winked at Thorn, and they descended, Violetta and Lord Sycamore following.

When they reached the bottom, the darkness deepened. Ping and Thorn snapped their fingers and clapped their hands, but their attempts to summon light were in vain.

Violetta wailed, "Oh dear, the magic fades here. We must turn back."

Ping asked, "Lord Sycamore, can you bring light?"

Lord Sycamore let out a weary sigh. "I can see nothing is going to deter you, Your Majesty."

"Nope, nothing. And please don't call me Your Majesty. Ping will do or call me Princess if you must remain so formal."

With a reluctant nod, Sycamore conjured a glowing orb with a wave of his hand, casting a warm light against the cold stone walls.

"Wow," Ping cried. "Can you show me how to do that?"

Thorn whispered, "It's difficult. I haven't fully mastered it yet, but sometimes I can make small orbs."

"That's helpful," Ping said.

No cells emerged, but a tunnel stretched before them. Lord Sycamore's orbs lit their path, revealing rough-hewn walls. The earthy scent of stone and soil lingered, adding to the eerie silence that enveloped them.

Violetta shivered, her voice a whisper. "The silence. It's spooky."

Ping patted her arm. "You can return if you wish, Violetta. But I must see every secret these dungeons hold."

She turned to Sycamore. "What was this level originally used for?"

"Perhaps, storage."

Violetta wrinkled her nose. "From all the dirt and dust, it seems nobody goes here."

Ping agreed. "No footprints, but faeries would fly, leaving no trace."

Lord Sycamore said, "Why would anyone come at all?"

"For the thrill of exploration?" Thorn suggested. "Who could resist such adventure?"

"Me," Violetta grumbled.

Ping's shoulders lifted in a hopeful shrug. "They might come seeking the portal. I'll bet it's at the end of the tunnel!"

Lord Sycamore folded his arms, and Ping prepared for another lecture. She quickly asked, "Did any of the stories reveal how to find the portal?"

He shook his head. "Not that I've ever heard."

At the tunnel's end, a wall blocked their way. Ping studied it. Same structure and texture as the tunnel. No buttons to push or levers to pull. As she stared at the unyielding wall, a sense of frustration washed over her.

Ping said, "Lord Sycamore, if you wanted to open a portal by magic, how would you go about it?"

"Princess, I've never needed to open a portal."

Ping continued to inspect the wall. "A tunnel needs a purpose, a destination. Why does this one just stop?"

Lord Sycamore speculated, "If it served as a storage entrance from outside, they could have sealed it once it became obsolete."

"That makes sense," Thorn said.

"That's true," Ping said. "But this tunnel is different. A secret hides here, I'm certain. I guess our journey ends here for now."

With a sense of unfulfilled curiosity, they retraced their steps, Lord Sycamore extinguishing the light orbs and leaving the tunnel to its eternal silence.

CHAPTER 23

An Attack and a Clue

Ping opened her chamber window to let in the evening breeze, carrying the sweet fragrance of the flowers in the garden below. Exhausted from her exploration of the dungeon's dim depths, Ping sought refuge in her luxurious bed. Her dreams tangled together, shrouded in gloom, and were haunted by a room filled with eerie shapes and shadows.

"Missy Ping, wake, wake, wake up!" a distant voice urged, a frantic cry that shattered her nightmare.

Ping's eyes whipped open to find a masked figure looming over her, pressing something down on her mouth. An unseen force restrained her hands, thwarting her fingers' efforts to snap for light. A sack thrust over her head plunged her world into darkness. Something wrapped around her body, squeezing her tight. She tried to scream, but the sack muffled her cries.

Help! Help! I'm under attack!

She was lifted, but then, the hands holding her loosened, and she dropped onto the bed.

A series of grunts, followed by a slap, slap, slap. Someone was being smacked, and it wasn't her!

"Argggg!" A cry of pain.

"Eeee! Squeak, Squeak! Squeeeeeal!"

Flap, flap, flap. Wings retreating.

Then silence.

The bindings imprisoning her twitched and loosened.

Ping's voice trembled. "Who's there?"

Her fear dissolved into relief as the sack over her head jiggled and was tugged away.

Chia's breath tickled her ear. "Princess, we are very, very, very sorry. We came as fast as we could. Are you hurt?"

Ping snapped her shaking fingers for light. "W-w-w-what happened?"

"We couldn't see who it was. I'm not sure who it even tasted like," Chia replied.

"Tasted?" Ping echoed, puzzled.

"Yes, we bit, bit, bit him fiercely! Our bites sent him fleeing. Peanut gave chase, but he kicked her before he took flight. She's shaken, but unharmed."

Tears of gratitude glistened in Ping's eyes as she surveyed her valiant rescuers—mice, rats, and spiders. "Oh, thank you all for saving me! This villain might be the one who took my mother and Zinnia. Without your bravery, I might have vanished, too!"

Chia nodded, brimming with pride. "The spiders spotted the danger and alerted me. I'm so glad you woke to my cry. Then we heard you shouting in our heads."

Ping stared. "In your heads?"

Before Chia could answer, a flurry of feathers filled the chamber as birds flocked through the open window. They all chirped at once until a bluebird's shrill whistle silenced them. "Princess Ping, are you well?" the bluebird asked. "Your distress call reached us."

"You heard me?"

"Yes, your call for help was clear."

Chia helped Ping explain what had happened.

The birds and critters scattered as the door was flung open and guards flew in, searching for danger.

Observing the chaos, the captain said, "Your Majesty, did those creatures attack you? Are you injured?"

Ping smiled. "I'm fine now. These friends saved me from an intruder."

The birds twittered among themselves.

"Friends?" the captain asked, confusion apparent on his face.

"Someone tried to kidnap me. I think he escaped through the window. Perhaps you could search?"

Tipping their wings, the guards rushed out.

Violetta zoomed in, eyes widening when she saw the visitors. "Princess, as soon as I heard your distress call, I alerted the guards!"

"Thank you, Violetta! It's over now. An intruder tried to kidnap me, but my friends here scared him away."

Ping scanned the room, her smile grateful for the

supportive gathering of crawling and flying creatures. "Thank you all for your help tonight."

"We'll post guards in your room at night," the bluebird said.

Chia nodded. "We'll do the same. You'll not be alone."

"That would ease my mind, but I fear it will be a burden to you."

The bluebird rustled her feathers. "Worry not. We are many, and we will take turns. It is no burden to care for our princess who calls us friend."

Ping smiled with gratitude. "Now that everything has calmed down, did anyone see my attacker?"

They all shook their tiny heads.

One plucky mouse piped up, "Perhaps a bite test is in order to find the one who tastes of betrayal."

"Oh, no!" Ping cried. "You mustn't nibble on innocent pixies." When she saw the tiny mouse's drooping whiskers, she said, "But thank you for the courageous suggestion."

"We got a good sniff," another mouse said. "We'll know if we smell him again."

"That's clever," Ping said. "I was so scared, I quite forgot to sniff."

Four mice settled under the bed and three birds settled themselves on the windowsill, tucking their heads beneath their wings.

Once snuggled under her covers, sleep evaded Ping, but the knowledge that she was now protected by the small warriors brought comfort to her heart.

The morning after the attack, Ping lingered by the window, enjoying her view of the garden below. Ping found renewed pleasure in Pixiandria's easy access to fresh air and sunshine. She savored the multicolored display of flowers swaying in the gentle morning breeze. This glorious faery world nourished her adventurous spirit. She shuddered as she realized someone had tried to take her away from it.

Ping had sent the birds and the mice who guarded her during the night on their way with the reassurance she'd be alert and watchful for danger. Her thoughts turned to musings about the intruder. Who was it? The guards found nobody in their search of the palace and grounds. Hopefully, the critter spies could sniff the kidnapper out.

Maybe she'd remember something that would help identify the assailant. Ping sifted through her memories of the night's terror, searching for a clue, a scent, anything that might reveal her attacker. He'd put his hand over her mouth. But her fright must have shut down her senses. She couldn't recall any smells or tastes. The cloth that had muffled her cries lay discarded on the floor. What did it smell like? She rushed over and put it to her nose. It had a distinct odor of cloth. Nothing else. Not much help.

The assailant was a giant compared to her petite frame, a shadowy adult figure. Was it someone she knew?

Thorn was an unlikely suspect, with his easy smile and small stature. She guessed he might have hired someone or had an accomplice. But why would he?

What would he have to gain from her disappearance? Nothing that she could see. He wasn't in line to gain the throne.

Lord Sycamore? Could he be the one? With her out of the way, the Kaboodle might choose him to rule the land. He was certainly a possibility.

But it also could be a stranger. Many unknown pixies surrounded her.

Rustling sounds behind her brought her attention to the corner of the room. She turned to see Chia scuttling across the floor, eagerness brightening his tiny eyes.

"I have news, Missy Ping. A spider spy reported that a couple of days ago—possibly the day Lady Zinnia disappeared—he was napping in the lower level. A faery disturbed him, carrying something heavy."

"Was the faery male or female?"

"He thought it might be a male. The spider's annoyance at being disturbed clouded his description."

"So, he didn't see a portal open?"

Chia's tiny body buzzed with irritation. "No, but the faery flew toward the dead end, and he didn't return."

Ping's heart warmed with gratitude for the information. "Thank you, Chia. This confirms the portal is in the dungeon and where it's located."

Chia nodded vigorously. "Yes, yes, yes, Missy Ping. I've doubled my spies in that area. They'll stay alert." Then he added, "Don't worry. The spiders and mice will keep to the shadows, guarding you today. They'll warn you if they smell the attacker."

Ping offered him a wedge of raspberry tart. Chia

plopped it into his backpack and skittered across the room, disappearing through the tiny crack in the wall.

She still knew little about the portal. How did it open? Where did it lead? Someone must know about the portal. But who?

Ping found Violetta sitting in a chair in the hallway guarding the grand wooden door to her chamber. "I stayed awake all night to protect my princess."

"My dear friend, I'm so sorry!" Ping cried. "You couldn't have been comfortable."

Violetta displayed the spirit of a tiny lioness. "Princess. I won't let anyone try to take you again."

While Violetta fetched tea to refresh them both, Ping slipped into an emerald gown woven with silvery ribbons she could tie without Violetta's help. She considered what to do next. The weight of the crown loomed heavy now that she realized someone wanted to keep her from it. Her journey to Pixiandria had begun with a kidnapping, and she had no desire to relive that experience. Helplessness did not suit her.

She'd never thought she was a leader. Frigg was the leader. All that responsibility! Frigg thrived on it. Being a follower was so much more fun. But Ping knew what Frigg would do. She'd act, rather than wait to be kidnapped again. It was time for Ping to forge her own path.

But where to begin?

Violetta's playful voice broke through Ping's thoughts. "Princess, your hair is a rainbow of emotions today. It's quite mesmerizing!"

Ping's cheeks warmed as she realized her curls had

been swirling with colors, reflecting the storm of her thoughts. "Sorry. Seems my emotions have taken control. I'll try to calm myself and my hair."

But peace proved difficult.

The portal must be the answer to finding her mother and Zinnia. Entering the Dark Lands was daunting, yes, but Ping was ready. She'd bravely confront it to restore her normal life.

The first step was clear: to unlock the portal's secrets. Someone held the key.

With a heart full of hope and a head full of unwavering blue hair, she decided to search her mother's chamber for hidden secrets. Among those secrets, she believed, lay a clue to her mother's vanishing.

CHAPTER 24

The Queen's Chamber

Ping squared her shoulders, bracing herself for the expected objections, and requested, "Violetta, would you accompany me to my mother's chamber?"

Violetta bit her lip. "Oh dear, I'm not sure we should go there while she's away."

"I disagree. I'm her daughter, after all. Who has a better right to be there than me?"

Violetta hesitated, her words trailing off. "It's just that..."

"Please, Violetta. I'd rather not order you to take me." She smiled, and the attendant smiled back nervously.

"Yes, Princess. I'll check with Daffodil. She'll want to be present."

"Daffodil?"

Violetta nodded. "Daffodil is the Queen's attendant. She's very protective of the Queen."

Ping let out a gentle sigh, turning her hair a deep purple of annoyance. "I'd hoped to keep my visit discreet, without stirring up palace rumors."

"I'm certain Daffodil would never gossip."

"Perhaps. But let's invite Daffodil here for a chat, shall we? Tea might warm her to the mission."

"A wonderful idea. I'll go right now."

Before long, she returned with a mature, silver-haired faery. Daffodil curtsied and tipped a wing with practiced ease. "Princess Peony, I'm at your service."

Ping greeted Daffodil with her most charming, but puzzled, smile. "Peony? You must have misheard. My name is Ping."

Daffodil's expression crinkled in surprise. "Glittering gadflies! Your mother, our beloved Queen Aster, gave you the name Peony."

"Peony?" Ping tried to hide her surprise. "I was unaware." Her thoughts raced at this news. She had another name! If pixie girls were named after flowers, it made sense she would have a flower name as well.

"I prefer to be called by the only name I have known."

Daffodil frowned but dipped in another curtsy. "Yes, Princess Ping, if that is your wish."

Ping nodded to Violetta, who left to prepare the tea. "It's a pleasure to meet you, Daffodil. I'd love to learn more about my mother. You've known her best."

Daffodil's cheeks flushed with honor. "Yes, Princess, I have served your mother since before you were born. I held you in my arms after you'd taken your first breath. You were such a darling baby, even with your tiny face all scrunched up in a cry."

A fond smile played on Daffodil's lips at the memory, then faltered. "Queen Aster was distraught when she had to send you away. We all were. The palace seemed so empty when you were gone. You were little, but a mighty force, and there was a toddler-sized hole in our hearts when you left."

Ping's voice was a whisper. "I thought I was alone in the world. I wish I had known so many caring faeries were here thinking about me."

A single tear escaped Daffodil's eye. Ping reached out, gently wiping the tear away.

Violetta returned with tea and blueberry tarts. They sat at the table and shared their tea, while Ping and Violetta entertained Daffodil with stories of Ping's tea parties with the birds and bees. Daffodil shared amusing tales of the Queen's trials and tribulations with the royal court.

As the stories faded away, Ping's mood turned solemn. "These memories make me feel closer to my mother."

"I'm so glad, Princess."

Ping continued. "Her portrait is lovely, but so grand and formal. It doesn't give a sense of who she really is. I'd love to visit her chamber to see how she lives and the objects she cherishes. Would you be my guide by showing me my mother's life?"

Daffodil's eyes shone with understanding. "Oh, yes, Princess. I'm not supposed to let anyone into her chamber. But you're her daughter. I think she'd approve."

And with a flutter of wings, Daffodil led the way to the Queen's chamber to reveal the memories held within. What had begun as a mission to uncover secrets had turned into a chance to discover Ping's early life.

As Ping and Daffodil approached the Queen's chamber, the air seemed to shimmer with anticipation. The grand doors, carved from ancient oak and inlaid with mother-of-pearl, swung open, revealing a massive room bathed in a soft glow. Ping stepped inside, her heart swelling with a desire to know the mother she had glimpsed only through a portrait and a few stories.

The chamber displayed both royal elegance and tranquil comfort. Velvet drapes in deep royal purples and blues cascaded from the tall windows. Silken tapestries adorned the walls, depicting the Queen's many adventures, each stitch telling a story of bravery and kindness. Ping realized her mother had lived an entire life her daughter knew nothing about.

Garlands of fresh flowers trailed from the ceiling, their scents delightful. A canopy bed stood in the center, its posts reaching toward the ceiling, carved with flower images. The bed, dressed in layers of gossamer linens and plush pillows, seemed to invite Ping to sink into dreams of a glamorous life lived.

To one side stood a wooden writing desk with intricate carvings on its front panel, mirroring those on the canopy posts. Waiting for the Queen's return, its surface was neatly covered with parchment stationery, ink bottles, and feather pens. A tower of large leather-bound books teetered on the edge. A crystal vase, dwarves shapeshifted, giving them newfound strength to fight the evil trolls. They'd fought alongside a diverse assembly of magical womenfolk. Even the mountain cave creatures—bats, spiders, and salamanders—had rallied together, united against the common enemy.

They'd beaten the trolls through sheer passion and righteous anger, but Ping knew that any future battles against invaders would require expertise. They were mastering those skills at Dagny's lessons.

Ping smiled as she thought about Frigg's mission convincing the Nadavir Council to build this school where girls of all backgrounds could learn together. Besides defense class, they had lessons in geography, universal language, literature, math, and science. Ainsel, Frigg's former tutor, was the headteacher—a wise choice, given Ainsel's vast knowledge and caring nature.

Ping's attention returned to Dagny, a courageous member of the Anasgar Dwarf Colony Guard, who'd volunteered to teach weaponry and defensive skills. When today's lesson ended, she gathered her charges and, like a seasoned general rallying her troops, sent them on their way, her inspiring words echoing through the cavern. "Stay strong and stay safe!"

From Ping's high perch, a loneliness gnawed at her heart as she watched the girls chattering. She knew if she flew down to Frigg's shoulder, she could join them. It might be fun. But there weren't any faeries to talk to.

Nadavir was a melting pot of magical folk who'd sought refuge in the dwarf colony from the humans spreading over the land. Yet Ping was the only pixie faery. She didn't know why faeries hadn't sought Nadavir. Maybe there weren't any faeries left. Maybe she was the last of her kind in the world. And how had she gotten to Nadavir? She'd been here as long as she could remember. It was a puzzle.

She'd thought about going out onto the surface to find other faeries, but where would she look? The books she'd read said faeries lived in barrow hills. These hills harbored a faery triad—oak, ash, and hawthorn trees—where faeries might reveal themselves. If you saw a faery triad, you'd have a better chance to see a faery. Ping had grown up inside caves, and simple drawings in books probably weren't enough to help her recognize those three trees.

She fluttered down to the giant weapons' trunk, where the other girls had stored their practice weapons. The lid was open, so she dove inside and tucked her pin in a back corner behind the swords, daggers, cudgels, bows, arrows, and hammers. As she examined the sheaths and scabbards protecting the other sharp implements, she tried to imagine what she could use to protect her pin.

THUMP! The trunk lid slammed shut.

The lock clicked.

Ping's tiny body was trapped within the pitch-black embrace of the trunk. Fumbling upward, she banged her fists against the unyielding lid. The girls' voices grew distant, unaware of her problem. She shouted and pounded until the voices faded into silence.

Ping froze, her body stiffening as she realized she was alone, locked inside a treasure chest brimming with weapons capable of destroying her wooden prison. But her pin, a skinny sliver of metal, was the only one she could lift. It wasn't big enough to smash anything. She might stick it through a crack in the wood, but what good would that do?

She was sure her hair had turned white with fear, and she wished it had the power to glow so she could see inside the trunk.

Her skin prickled, as if ghostly insects crawled over her. Imaginary? A shuddering coldness settled in her belly as she slumped against something that felt like a sword hilt.

"Stay calm," she urged herself. "All will be well. I'm safe inside this trunk."

Her words helped control her panic.

Faery dust! Clutching her necklace, she opened the stopper of the tiny bottle of faery dust she'd scraped from colorful rocks and poured some into her hand. Tossing the dust toward the lid, she shouted, "Open!"

The lid didn't budge, but the dust made her sneeze.

Ping huffed with resignation. She was stuck. Nothing to do but wait until Dagny opened the trunk tomorrow morning.

She settled into her wooden cocoon, twiddling her thumbs.

She hummed her favorite song, the lilting melody soothing her tensions.

She told herself a story about a beautiful faery who magically grew and punched her way out of a trunk to freedom.

She brought visions to her mind of the adventures

she'd experienced. The terrifying and wondrous moments she'd shared with Frigg, Tip, and Cricall on their quest to find the Anasgar dwarf colony. Who knew that a faery, dwarf, elf, and unicorn would make an incredible team? Each memory of their journey had etched itself into her heart.

She sighed. Yet here she was, alone.

Her eyelids drooped, and she must have dozed, because she awakened to a scratching sound. Was it rescue? Had Frigg traced her back to class?

She pounded hard on the lid, bellowing for help. Her voice echoed inside the trunk's wooden chamber. "Hey, I'm in here. Let me out!"

The lock clicked, and the lid lifted from Ping's clenched fists. After the trunk's inky blackness, she squinted against the blinding brightness of the glow-worm's wall sconce, bathing the room with light. She blinked rapidly as her eyes adjusted.

Her heartbeat quickened at the illusion before her—a radiant pixie faery hovered beside the trunk lid, waving a wand.

CHAPTER 2

It's All Relative

A pixie? It couldn't be! Was she dreaming? She must be seeing things again! But this faery wasn't hiding in the corner of Ping's eye. Glowing strands of brilliant red hair danced around her shoulders like flame-kissed silk. Her slender wings, reminding Ping of a dragonfly, fluttered delicately behind her.

"W-w-who are you?" Ping stammered.

The faery's wand disappeared with a flick of her wrist. "I'm your Aunt Iris and I've come to take you home."

Ping's mind spun in a whirlwind. "My Aunt Iris? Home? Huh?"

The faery hovering before her waggled her head and the teeny blue flowers adorning her red hair bounced. "I suppose this requires some explaining, doesn't it?"

Ping's buzzing thoughts left her speechless, but a sudden realization struck her. "You're what I've been seeing from the corner of my eye!"

Iris ducked her head. "Yes, I'm usually more careful when I come to check on you."

"I'm glad I'm not imagining things. Wait, you've been here before?"

Iris's wings fluttered. "Yes, I come often to make sure you're still alive and well. You always are. Alive and well, that is. But I keep checking anyway. I brought you to the dwarves when you were a small child. To keep you safe, you know."

Ping's brow furrowed. "Safe? From the humans?"

A chuckle escaped Aunt Iris. "No, silly girl! From the evil faery who was attacking your mother. But I guess you wouldn't recall that because I erased your memory."

Eyes widening, Ping's hands clenched into fists, turning her knuckles white. "You erased my memory? Why?"

"So you wouldn't remember the evil faery who threatened your mother."

Ping's hair turned as red as her face. "That's no reason to erase my memory! What else don't I remember?"

Aunt Iris crossed her arms and sighed. "I suppose I should start at the beginning."

"Yes, I think you should."

Suddenly, the door creaked open, and Frigg's voice called out across the cavernous practice room, "Ping, are you in here?"

"Yes, Frigg!" Ping called. "Come quick! You won't believe who's here."

Panic flashed across Iris's face. "No! She shouldn't see me."

Ping gripped her arm and held on tight. "She's my best friend. You're safe with her."

Iris didn't appear convinced.

Frigg rushed to the trunk, her eyes widening as she took in the scene. "Galloping garnets! Who's this?"

Ping's grin widened, revealing her tiny, sparkling teeth. "Frigg, I'd like you to meet my Aunt Iris, or at least that's who she claims to be. Aunt Iris, this is my best friend, Frigg."

"Pleased to meet you," Frigg said, glancing between Ping and Iris. "Where did you come from?"

"From Pixiandria, of course," Aunt Iris snapped, her tone sharp as a thorn. "Where else would a pixie come from?"

"That's kinda rude," Ping said. "She asked you a perfectly reasonable question. Where exactly is Pixiandria, anyway?"

Iris huffed and wiggled her fingers. "It's over that way. About two clegs by bird flight."

"Clegs?" Ping raised an eyebrow. Her hair had softened from red to a pale lavender.

"Never mind. The important thing is that I need to take you home to Pixiandria. We must present you to the court or that dreadful Zinnia will take the queenship. When you're settled on the throne, we'll unravel the mystery of Aster's disappearance and rescue her. If she's still alive, that is."

Frigg and Ping exchanged confused glances.

Ping's hair shifted to a deep shade of purple, and she rubbed her cheeks in exasperation. "Hold on, that was gibberish! Who are Zinnia and Aster? What's this queenship business? And why do I need a throne?"

Iris exhaled with a whoosh. "It's a rather long story, my dear. But before I spill the pixie beans, my throat's parched. A decent story requires tea and nourishment."

Frigg jumped to attention. "Blundering bloodstones! How silly of me not to have invited you home for dinner. That's why I came looking for Ping. Dinner is ready. Would you like to join us?" She turned to Ping. "Mom invited Tip. He's going to love this fresh development."

Iris, indecision filling her narrowed eyes, curtsied gracefully in midair. "I guess that would be lovely." A wand appeared in her hand and with a wave, the trunk lid slammed shut and locked. "Lead the way."

Off they went, leaving behind a trail of curiosity and magic in their wake. In the tunnels that snaked through the ancient rock of the Nadavir dwarf colony, magical folk paused in their work. Their eyes widened as they watched Frigg darting through the passages with two teeny faeries gliding above her, their wings shimmering like spun silver in the gleam of the glow-worm lanterns. Two faeries!

Ping smiled at their surprised faces and waved. Accustomed to seeing Ping flitting about alone, this new pixie companion must be a delightful mystery.

They emerged from the shadows outside their home cave. An elf, lounging against a mossy boulder, blinked and waggled his head as though clearing his vision. Tip focused on the unfamiliar figure flying beside Ping. In a voice hushed with wonder, he said to

Ping, "Who is this mysterious stranger?"

Ping zipped to his ear and gave it an affectionate pinch.

Tip flinched. "Ow! Stop that!"

Ping shrugged, mischief dancing in her eyes. "But it's our special signal."

"Signal for what?" Tip grumbled.

"Signal I'm here!"

"I can see you're here." He rubbed his ear. "You don't have to squeeze my ear off!"

Frigg sighed. "Enough, you two. Tip, meet Ping's Aunt Iris."

"Ping has an aunt?" Tip raised a curious eyebrow. "Well, this is unexpected."

Frigg continued the introductions. "Iris, meet Tip, our friend."

Iris tilted her head, eyes sparkling. "An elf! How unusual. Nice to meet you, Tip."

"I'm glad you're here," Ping said to Tip. "Now you can hear my aunt's story, along with the rest of us."

Tip studied Iris, intrigue etching his features. "Yes, I think there's probably an interesting tale here.

Frigg took charge. "C'mon, let's go tell Ma and Birgit we've got another guest for dinner."

After Frigg's mother, Namis, grasped the idea that Ping had an aunt, she greeted Iris warmly. Their housekeeper, Birgit, rushed to arrange another place at the table. As they settled down to eat, Dvalin, Frigg's father, raised his tankard in a toast to unexpected friendships.

Tip shouted, "Let the discoveries begin!"

CHAPTER 3

What a Story!

Surrounded by a table filled with mushroom stew and freshly baked bread, Iris shared her tale. Everyone leaned forward, their eyes locked on her, eager to unravel the mysteries that had been hidden for so long. As she spoke, the crackling fire echoed through the room, creating a cozy mood.

"Before I brought Ping here, chaos reigned in Pixiandria, the heart of our pixie realm."

"Pixiandria?" Namis asked. "Is that where you live?"

Iris nodded, her eyes alight. "Indeed, it's our pixie homeland."

Ping imagined the vibrant colors of the pixie realm as Iris described it—the lush greens of the meadows, the sparkling blues of the rivers, and the warm hues of the setting sun. "A homeland." Ping sighed and her hair blushed pink with excitement.

"But all was not well in Pixiandria," Iris continued.

"Queen Aster, who is my sister and Ping's mother, ruled with an iron will. You see, when humans took over the land, Pixies thought they could make them leave with pixie pranks—souring their milk, leading their sheep astray, and snarling their hair while they slept."

Dvalin scowled. "Doesn't seem very neighborly."

Iris's gaze held a hint of mischief. "True, but these were our pixie traditions until Queen Aster banned them. She decided humans were much too dangerous to trick. She ordered all pixies to stay away from humans, lest we provoke their wrath."

"Quite logical." Dvalin nodded. "We're following a similar strategy here in Nadavir—steering clear of humans."

Frigg said, "The pixies didn't like that?"

"They weren't happy, not at all."

Ping snorted. "I guess I can understand that. Sounds like they were enjoying their little tricks."

Iris's eyes gleamed. "Lady Zinnia disagreed and declared Queen Aster's ideas insulting. She said we had to fight to reclaim our lands from the humans."

Tip interrupted. "Who's Lady Zinnia?"

Iris's upper lip curled. "Ah, she's our pixie kaboodle's most vexing member. She dreams of being a queen, but we already have a queen. That puts a crimp in her ambitions."

"I see," Dvalin said. "She'd naturally oppose the Queen's rulings."

Iris nodded. "Oh yes. Lady Zinnia's disapproval of Queen Aster's opinions is as predictable as the sunrise."

Dvalin chuckled. "Indeed, ambition has no limits in any realm."

"Anyway," Iris went on. "Queen Aster said that the humans who trampled our meadows and disturbed our magic were too big to defeat."

Intrigue shone in Frigg's eyes as she leaned in closer. "Seems like wise advice."

As Iris spoke, tiny sparks danced in the air. "Yes, but Zinnia argued that humans lacked magic. Since we wield the earth's magic, we were stronger."

Ping's curiosity burst forth. "Do I have earth magic?"

"Indeed, little one, you do," Iris assured her.

Namis patted Ping's hand. "I know you're eager to learn about your magic, Ping, but let's allow Iris to share her story first."

Iris rushed to continue. "Where was I? Oh, yes, Zinnia relentlessly opposed Aster, calling her weak and insisting we had to prove our strength by conquering the humans. She gave a grand speech, saying, 'We pixies, the smallest of the faeries, shall become the mightiest.'"

Ping's heart raced, her tiny wings quivering with a mix of excitement and fear.

Tip opened his mouth to speak, but Dvalin gave him a stern look.

Iris said, "They argued, their words striking like arrows. Eventually, the fight went beyond words. Zinnia challenged Aster to a series of wand duels." Iris soared above the table, a wand appearing in her hand. She swished and dodged as an imaginary foe attacked and sparks flew from the wand.

Namis cried, "Oh my!"

Dvalin said, "Thank you, Iris. I think we get the point."

Iris blushed and returned to her seat. "In every confrontation, Aster prevailed, but her strength dwindled. She feared where Zinnia's fury might lead. At the heart of everything lay tiny Ping—only a toddler, but the key to Pixiandria's destiny. If Aster died, Ping would become queen. We worried what Zinnia might do to Ping to remove her from the royal succession."

Frigg jumped to her feet, upsetting her stew bowl. "That's horrible. Why would anyone hurt an innocent child?"

The room fell into hushed silence, everyone appearing to hold their breath.

Iris trembled as she recounted the moment Queen Aster came to her and, with tears in her eyes, begged Iris to protect Ping.

As Iris described Queen Aster's tears, Ping could almost taste the bittersweetness of sacrifice and the unbreakable bond of sisterhood.

Iris twisted her hands, her eyes haunted. "My sister said, 'Ping is the pixies' future. If I'm defeated, Zinnia's followers will hunt her down.'"

"How cruel!" Tip cried. "What kind of land is Pixiandria?"

"It can be brutal when faeries vie for power. I was terrified. I'm one pixie with laughable fighting skills. How could I protect Ping?"

Tip leaned forward, bobbing his head. "I think I see where this story is headed."

"SHHH!" Everyone hushed him.

Iris pressed on. "Aster's solution was both desperate and brilliant. She urged me to hide Ping until she grew to rise and rule. My instructions were to tell nobody, not even Aster. I was to seek those who'd raise her as their own, far from Zinnia's reach. The rumor of Ping's kidnapping would spread. When they failed to find her, they'd give up."

Tears trickled down Iris's cheeks as she gazed at Ping. Her voice cracked. "I was scared, Ping. Scared that I wouldn't be able to keep you safe. I couldn't bear the weight of such a responsibility, but it was my burden, my challenge."

Iris's next words pierced the air. "I fled to the nursery, scooped Ping from her oak-leaf crib, and soared from the palace. Perched high in my favorite twisty hawthorn tree, I searched for an answer. How could I shield Ping from the dark forces gathering under Lady Zinnia's banner? Where could I take a small child? Where would she be safe?"

Iris paused. The dining room fell silent, everyone absorbing the remarkable tale—the missing pieces of Ping's origin slotting into place. "I remembered hearing about a sanctuary where the pixie princess might hide, far from her enemies' clutches."

"Where? Where?" Tip's eyes sparkled with curiosity.

Laughter erupted, breaking the tension. Iris flitted across the table and patted Tip's cheek. "Why, right here, silly elf," she said. "I brought her to safety with the dwarves of Nadavir."

As Ping listened to her own story—the twists and

turns that had led her to this cozy hearth—she observed Frigg's father. Dvalin's eyebrows danced—a silent conversation with his thoughts.

"Ah," Dvalin said, "this is where I come in. Hilla found Ping under a tree outside and brought her to me. All the little faery said was one word—Ping. We couldn't figure out what it meant or where she came from."

She'd waited for these answers all her life. Like a sprinkle of pixie dust, the truth revealed that Ping had an unknown enemy plotting her demise in Pixiandria. It felt too dramatic, too impossible, too unwanted.

"And now," Iris concluded with an anxious gaze around the table. "Queen Aster has vanished. Poof! Gone without a trace. We have to return home immediately. Ping must claim the throne."

"Immediately?" Ping's mind raced with questions and emotions as she tried to understand her destiny. She needed time to grasp all she'd heard.

"Yes, right away, as in now!" Iris's eyes blazed with urgency. "No time to lose. When your mother returns, she must find you holding onto the throne. What's most important is that the pixies need to become accustomed to you as their future ruler, especially if Aster doesn't return."

Namis asked, "Do you think the Queen might not come back?"

Iris hesitated, her gaze resting on Ping. "There's always that possibility. But we won't think about that. She will return. And when she does, she'll see you protecting your birthright."

CHAPTER 4

Pros and Cons

Ping took a deep breath, twirling a strand of lavender hair around her finger. She had so much to think about! This morning, she had no faery family. Now, she had a faery family, but she'd lost her mother before she ever knew her. Her aunt wanted to take her to Pixiandria to lead the faery folk she knew nothing about. Oh, and her enemies might kill her. This wasn't exactly what she'd expected when she'd wished for other pixies in Nadavir!

Frigg jumped in. "Ping needs time. You've just sprung this on her. She can't leave Nadavir unprepared."

Tip leaned closer to Ping, his voice hushed. "What are you thinking, Ping? This entire story is pretty incredible. Are you okay?"

A bit overwhelmed, Ping smiled at Frigg and Tip. They always knew when Ping needed support. "I'm not sure what to think."

"No time for preparation," Iris declared. "I'll brief her as we fly. Two doves await in a tree outside Nadavir. We'll ride them to Pixiandria."

Dvalin raised a bushy eyebrow. "Doves?"

"Pixiandria is quite far. The palace guards ride ravens, but I find doves gentler. Our wings would wilt from exhaustion if we flew ourselves. So, riding doves, it is!" Iris paused. "Besides, we must save our strength for the battle ahead."

"Battle?" Frigg cried. "You didn't mention a battle."

Iris paused. "Well, perhaps battle is a tad dramatic. Let's call it a fight—a challenge we must face."

"But fight sounds just as bad!" Tip protested.

Namis, who had been silent, shook her head. "No, Ping can't possibly go alone to fight a battle!"

"I agree." Dvalin scowled. "I won't allow it. Ping isn't ready to face an experienced foe. She's still learning to fight. If she goes, we'll send dwarves along to assist her."

Ping muttered, "I've fought trolls. I think I can handle another pixie."

Frigg leaned forward. "Defending against the trolls, we had numbers and surprise on our side. This time, it's different. Iris, will the other pixies rally behind Ping?"

Iris's gaze dropped. "Well, the other pixies don't exactly know Ping is alive."

Tip sighed. "Shouldn't someone have told them?"

Iris hesitated, then confessed, "I'm the only one who knew, oh, and a few trusted palace servants. I told them to spread the word that I was leaving and would bring back a surprise."

Seeing the shock on the faces around the table, she added, "But I'm sure people have figured it out by now. Of course, they won't know where I went, but they'll probably guess the surprise is someone who can face that nasty old Zinnia."

Ping let out a weary groan. "Does Zinnia know about me?"

Iris laughed. "No, you're the surprise, remember?"

Dvalin's voice rumbled. "If this Zinnia has figured out Ping is alive, she'll be ready for her! We must dispatch dwarf scouts to investigate. Then we can decide our next move."

Iris soared to Dvalin and poked his nose. "You can't send dwarves to Pixiandria. The guards' magic won't let them in. Only pixies can enter through the enchanted borders. Rules, you know."

"But Da's right," Frigg said. "If Ping faces danger, she'll need friends. I must go with her. My fighting skills have improved. We can enlist Dagny and the other females to shapeshift into pixies. It'll look better for Ping if she has followers to lead into Pixiandria."

"Brilliant!" Tip cried.

Iris's expression turned serious. "You wouldn't get past the barrier if you've used magic to shift forms. We must slip into Pixiandria undetected by Zinnia's soldiers and confront her in court. It's our only chance."

"Stop! It's too much!" Ping's red hair swirled willy-nilly as she charged toward the door.

"Wait..." Iris shouted.

Ping didn't wait. She darted away. Her heart raced, and the weight of unwanted responsibility pressed upon her.

As Ping slipped into the bedroom she shared with Frigg, her wings fluttered with uncertainty. She made a beeline for Glimmer's lantern, its soft glow beckoning like a familiar friend. With deft fingers, she unlatched the tiny door.

"Hello, friend," Ping whispered, tickling the glow worm until he shimmered brightly. His gentle light always eased her, and right now, she needed any comfort available.

"What do you think I should do?" she asked Glimmer, knowing he couldn't offer a spoken answer. But sometimes, in their shared silent moments, she felt he understood her heart.

Glimmer vibrated, his glow pulsing in time with her heartbeat. Their eyes met in a silent exchange.

"Perhaps you do understand," Ping murmured.

"If I go with Iris, I'd get to see the homeland I've never known. I'd also get to meet other pixies like me. Isn't that what I've always longed for? But it's dangerous. I have enemies I didn't know existed."

Glimmer wiggled, glowing brighter, as if urging her on.

"If I stay, I'll be surrounded by people who care for me. But I'll never glimpse the lives of other faeries, never know their secrets or their magic."

Glimmer's light dimmed, mirroring Ping's uncertainty.

Ping reached into her dress pocket, retrieving a tiny notebook she'd crafted herself. She'd torn squares from Frigg's school paper, binding them with a dab of honey. With a makeshift coal pen, she wrote,

Go to Pixiandria

YES
1. Learn about my homeland and family.
2. May meet my mother if she's still alive.
3. Know other pixies.

NO
  1. Nobody knows about me, and everyone   might hate me.
  2. Dangerous! Risk of death.
  3. If I survive and defeat Zinnia, and stay in Pixiandria, I might have to rule an unfamiliar land.
  4. I don't know how to be a queen.
  5. Will I like it there?
  6. I'd miss Frigg, Cricall, and even Tip.
  7. And yes, IT'S DANGEROUS!

Ping studied the list, her heart fluttering like a moth drawn to Glimmer's light. No doubt about it, the Nos were beating out the Yeses. Doubt gnawed at her brain.

She flipped to the beginning of her notebook where she had been jotting down her Faery Rules. Because she didn't know how faeries were supposed to live, she'd been making up her own guidelines for being a faery. Maybe the sixteen rules she had so far would help her decide.

1. Don't mess with a faery.
2. Faery dust works when it feels like it.
3. A faery does what she wants, when she wants.
4. A faery's hair color reflects her mood.
5. Don't question the colors.

6. Faeries are unique.

7. Faeries won't be a nuisance to those they like.

8. Faeries will be a nuisance to those who are rude.

9. A Faery Triad is a circle of oak, ash, and haw-thorn trees and is a portal to the Faery World.

10. A faery must dance every day.

11. A faery must befriend messenger mice. They know all the best gossip!

12. Get outside and fly with the birds whenever possible.

13. Eat a honeycake each day to make you sweet.

14. A faery must make faery dust by scraping col-ored rocks. (See Rule #2.)

15. When others are sad, a faery giggle can change their mood.

16. Faeries keep their promises and protect their friends.

She added the two rules she'd learned in today's lesson:

17. Up, down, zig zag evades enemies in a fight.

18. Wave and Jab as a last resort.

The new ones might come in handy if she faced Zinnia in Pixiandria, but she thought rule number three held the answer. A faery does what she wants, when she wants.

What did she want? She wanted to know who she really was and where she came from. She'd braved danger before, but in Pixiandria, her friends wouldn't be there to back her up. Yet if she stayed, she'd always wonder what she'd missed.

CHAPTER 5

What Do the Runes Say ?

Agentle creak announced the bedroom door open-ing, and Frigg tiptoed in. "A lot to take in, huh?" she said, her eyes searching Ping's face.

"That's an understatement," Ping replied, her fingers tracing a mushroom pattern on her quilt. "I was trying to figure out where my true home is."

Frigg nodded, her blonde hair catching the glow filtering from Glimmer's lantern. "Nadavir will always be your home, Ping. You grew up here, and we're your family. But perhaps your heart can embrace two homes."

Ping hesitated. "I love Nadavir and never thought I'd leave it. But I'm curious about Pixiandria. I'm lonely here sometimes, being the only one of my kind."

Frigg studied her friend, her eyes wide with sur-prise. "I never knew, Ping. You hid it well. It makes sense you'd want to know about faeries. I've grown up surrounded by dwarves."

They sat in silence. After a moment, Ping said, "Should I go, Frigg?"

"That's a decision you have to make. I don't want you to go away, but I also don't want to hold you back."

"I was afraid you'd say that." Ping pointed to the small, black pouch resting on the shelf by Frigg's bed. "Will you read the runes for me?"

Frigg's lips twitched. "I'm no expert, but let's try to unravel fate together."

"You sound like Hilla," Ping said with a giggle, wondering if the runes would reveal answers to her questions.

Frigg squeezed the shapes within the black runes pouch, its worn fabric offering secrets of ages past. Hilla, the ancient Nadavir Oracle, had etched the rune symbols onto small, flat stones—each one a portal to fate. When Frigg was held captive at the freak show, she'd burned runes into wooden discs to dazzle the humans. However, this pouch with its carved stone images held more weight than mere wood.

She carefully unfolded the spotless white cloth, spreading it flat onto the bed. "When Hilla reads my runes, I hold the pouch and ask for the gods' guidance. Then I toss the runes onto the cloth. The runes are too heavy for your tiny hands to lift. If I do it, I think it would tell my future."

Ping said, "Let's do it together. Our hands touching the pouch, our minds asking the question."

Frigg's sturdy grip enveloped Ping's delicate fingers. Together, they said, "Odin and Freya, guide us. Should Ping journey to Pixiandria with Aunt Iris?"

The runes tumbled forth, clattering against each other as they hit the cloth. Frigg plucked out the ones that landed face down and returned them to the bag. She placed the face-up runes on the cloth, rearranging them into a square pattern.

She pointed. "That's Perth. It means good or bad luck, but it promises surprises. Whatever path you choose, expect twists and turns along the way."

Perth

With a crinkled nose, Ping's hair took on a worried yellow hue. "Surprises, huh? Iris's visit was a shock. Finding a new family was unexpected. What other surprises await?"

Frigg leaned closer, examining the runes with their ancient wisdom. "That's why they're called surprises. Hilla always says true magical surprises lie within your heart."

She picked up another rune. "Thurisaz means change."

Ping laughed. "Going to Pixiandria would be a huge change."

Thurisaz

Ping leaped up, brimming with energy. "But is it an opportunity or a danger? Like stepping into a fairy ring—delightful, yet risky."

Frigg shrugged. "Both? The runes weave tales, but the ending is yours to write."

Ping smiled. "You're sounding like Hilla again." She pointed to another rune. "What's this one?"

Raido

"Raido, journey. This one came up a lot on our trip to Anasgar. It could mean traveling to Pixiandria, or perhaps it's this journey of deciding whether to go."

"It could mean I'm taking a journey outside to wave goodbye to Iris," Ping mused, her heart fluttering like her butterfly wings.

Frigg chuckled. "That's one possibility! The one next to it is Kenaz. It's fire or light. It brings knowledge. You've already achieved this one. You have new information about your origins."

"Yes," Ping agreed. "The question is, how much more do I want to know about that?"

Kenaz

"This one is interesting," Frigg continued. "Algiz, the shield rune, offers protection. I don't see it often. It suggests defending yourself or others."

Algiz

Ping's mind raced. "Against Zinnia, perhaps?"

"You're a princess, Ping. Despite your concerns, being a princess is part of you now. Pixiandria needs a guardian. Possibly that someone is you."

"But how?" Ping's voice trembled. "I can't wield a sword or command armies."

Frigg rested her finger on Ping's shoulder, a comforting weight. "Perhaps," she said, "the answer lies in the knowledge you'll gain. You've trained and honed your skills. The gods have been whispering secrets to you, preparing you for a battle beyond steel—a battle of hearts and wings."

"I don't think I know how to do that," Ping whispered.

Frigg's voice softened. "I don't know, either. When we were in Anasgar, Dagny told me courage sometimes blooms in the most unexpected places. The runes offer a map to the unknown. Perhaps the smallest wings can carry the greatest hope."

She pointed to the next rune. "This one couldn't be much clearer. Othila means ancestry, like your family and home."

Othila

"Yes," Ping said, "But I have two families now. Which family is it referring to? Which home?

"Both? You must decide where to dig for your roots."

Frigg held the last rune on the cloth. This is Mannaz.

Mannaz

"I like this one," Ping said. "What does the X in the middle mean?"

"It represents mankind."

Tiny fists clenched, Ping protested, "Men, men, men! Don't the runes know I'm not a man?"

"Not one man, mankind. It includes everyone."

"I think it should be called everyonekind!"

Frigg laughed. "I agree. Let's rename it. Hilla told me to think about teamwork. A group of individuals working together for the common good."

"A group in Nadavir or in Pixiandria?" Ping asked.

"I'm guessing both. But since our question to the runes was about your birth land, it probably means Pixiandria."

Ping nodded, her wings fluttering. "Okay, we've got

a group of individuals working together for the common good in Pixiandria. Why would they need me?"

Frigg sprang to her feet. "Perhaps you're the missing piece, the one who brings them together. Sounds like they've been in conflict for a long time. Without you, they remain scattered like fallen leaves in the forest. You're an outsider with deep kinship to them. As much as I don't want you to go because I'll miss you, I think Pixiandria needs you. Everyonekind can't heal without a faery like you."

Nordic Runes of Nadavir

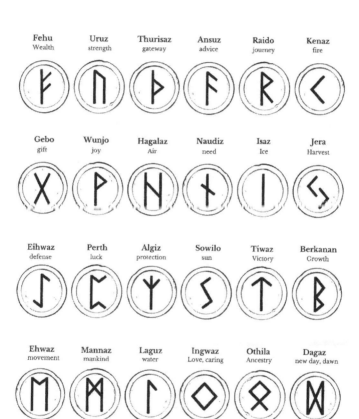

Fehu Wealth	**Uruz** strength	**Thurisaz** gateway	**Ansuz** advice	**Raido** journey	**Kenaz** fire

Gebo gift	**Wunjo** joy	**Hagalaz** Air	**Naudiz** need	**Isaz** Ice	**Jera** Harvest

Eihwaz defense	**Perth** luck	**Algiz** protection	**Sowilo** sun	**Tiwaz** Victory	**Berkanan** Growth

Ehwaz movement	**Mannaz** mankind	**Laguz** water	**Ingwaz** Love, caring	**Othila** Ancestry	**Dagaz** new day, dawn

33

CHAPTER 6

Ping Decides

Ping and Frigg returned to the dining room. The flickering flames of the hearth fire had died down, casting long shadows in the room, a reminder that time was running out. Iris, Dvalin, Namis, Birget, and Tip still gathered around the table, their expressions a mix of concern and curiosity. The air hummed with anticipation.

Ping didn't make them wait any longer. Turning to Iris, she said, "Yes, I will go with you to Pixiandria. What do I need to bring?"

"Nothing," Iris said, flying to her and wrapping her in an enormous hug. "Come as you are."

Dvalin rubbed his bushy beard and cleared his throat. "Ping, I don't think this is wise. As your guardian…"

Ping darted to him, interrupting with a kiss to his weathered cheek. Then she floated in front of him.

"You're a wonderful guardian. You've protected me and kept me safe." She peered around at the others. "You're an amazing family. Birgit, you've raised me to be responsible and trustworthy. Namis, you've treated me as a daughter since your return, and I've grown to love you. Tip, you've been a worthy, if annoying, friend. But none of you can teach me how to be a faery. In Pixiandria, I'll learn what it means to be what I was born to be—a true pixie."

Dvalin's gaze held hers, a silent understanding passing between them. "I'm sure your aunt will do everything she can to safeguard your journey. She was smart enough to bring you here to us." He paused and locked eyes with Iris, who blushed and nodded emphatically. Message received.

Crossing the room, Dvalin's gnarled hands retrieved a tiny bundle from a hidden drawer. I intended to give this to you during the Autumn Equinox, but you may find it useful now. He held out the bundle to Ping.

Tip sprang to his feet. "Open it!"

Unwrapping the treasure, Ping's breath caught when she saw a pixie-sized dagger encased by a sheath attached to a small belt. The dagger's handle nestled perfectly in her palm. She turned it over, the azure gemstones embedded in its hilt winking like a glow-worm's light. Her hands trembled at its beauty.

"For me?" she asked, gazing at Dvalin in wonderment.

"Absolutely," he said with a laugh. "Mift, our best metalsmith, made it to my special order just for you. He said he'd created nothing so delicate before. It may be small, but it's strong."

Ping buckled the belt around her waist. She flew to Dvalin and touched his wrinkled cheek. "Thank you. It's beautiful!"

Dvalin patted her back with his finger.

Around the table, everyone brushed away tears.

"Enough blubbering!" Frigg said, her voice wobbling. "Oh, Ping, I can't believe you're leaving. I wish I could join you. You've been my rock."

Ping turned to Iris. "Isn't there some way Frigg can come?"

Iris shook her head gently. "No, my dear. This journey is ours alone."

"Well, if I can't come, at least I'm going to see you off," Frigg said.

"Me, too," came a familiar voice from the entrance. Cricall, his majestic unicorn horn scraping the doorframe, said, "You wouldn't think of leaving without saying goodbye, would you?"

Ping darted to Cricall, hugging his velvety ear. "How did you know?"

Cricall snorted. "Tip dispatched a messenger mouse telling me to come. And now, here I am, stunned that you'd embark on a journey without us!"

"Cricall, I'm sorry! This journey has been sudden. Tip will explain everything later."

Upon seeing Iris's puzzled expression, Ping felt compelled to explain. "Cricall is a wonderful friend and was vital in our mission to find Anasgar. His healing powers saved my life."

"And what about me?" Tip asked.

Ping flew to Tip and flicked his ear playfully.

"Hey, what was that for?" he cried.

"For old times' sake," Ping said with a giggle. "A flick to remember me by."

Ping circled the room, sharing goodbyes. "I'm going to miss you all." With her new dagger at her waist, Ping and Iris led their supporters through Nadavir's winding tunnels. The air shifted from damp to crisp as they neared the mountain's mouth, filling their nostrils with the refreshing scent of pine.

Emerging into the moonlight outside the mountain, Iris snapped her delicate fingers and whistled. Nothing happened. "Strange," she murmured, her brow furrowing. "The doves should be waiting in that ancient oak." She gestured toward the gnarled tree, its twisted branches stretching skyward.

Everyone followed her gaze to the tree, but no white birds perched there. The silence hung heavy, broken only by rustling leaves and a distant bird call. They searched the sky for the doves that were supposed to carry Ping and Iris to Pixiandria.

Like a shockwave, the air exploded with a cacophony of screeches and flapping wings. Hundreds of shadowy forms swirled overhead, blotting out the moonlight and creating a whirlwind of feathers and threat.

Panic surged through the group as Iris, eyes wide, shouted. "The ravens! Run!"

CHAPTER 7

Surprise!

Despite Iris's cry to run, everyone's feet seemed rooted to the ancient earth.

Disoriented, Ping searched frantically in all directions for escape.

Birgit let out a primal scream that echoed through the gnarled trees.

Namis cradled her distress like a fragile bird. Her sobs mingled with the wind.

Tip, wide-eyed and disbelieving, stared at the unfolding scene.

Cricall unleashed a powerful roar.

Dvalin sprang into action. His brawny arms reached for the group, gathering them close. "To the entrance!" he commanded.

But his actions were too late.

Hundreds of black ravens swooped from the sky and surrounded them. The overwhelming chaos of dark shapes and cawing birds left them feeling helpless.

Someone seized Ping's arm and lifted her. It happened so fast she hadn't had time to cry out. The ground vanished, replaced by the cold, feathered back of a massive raven. Its rider held her in front of him with an iron grip. The night's blackness, along with the birds' dark wings, blocked out the moonlight, and Ping couldn't see more than enormous dark shapes around her. Her raven's wings pulsed, carrying her higher, and they soared away from Nadavir.

Panic clawed at her chest as she screamed out her frustration and fright. Would she ever see her home and her friends again? Desperation fueled Ping. She kicked her legs and shouted, "Put me down!"

Nobody replied. She continued to scream and kick.

Finally, the deep voice of the rider holding her laughed and shouted above the noise of the flapping wings. "I don't think you'd like it much if I put you down here. Water surrounds us. Can you swim, my little pet?"

"I'm not your pet!" Ping's defiance rang out. She hoped her hair had turned as red as her rage, even though he couldn't see it in this darkness. "Return me to Nadavir immediately."

"Well, Your Majesty, your wish is not my command. At least not until you wear the crown. I suggest you settle back and enjoy the ride."

Ping weighed her options. The rider was slightly larger than she was and much stronger, so she wouldn't win a struggle with him. Screaming hadn't worked. So, she silently clung to the raven's back, heart pounding, and wondered what fate awaited her at the end of their ride.

Her mind raced, weaving threads of possibility. He knew who Ping was, addressing her as "Your Majesty." What did he want?

She glanced around at the massive birds, wings flapping in unison. A little moonlight was now shining through the gloom as the ravens spread out. Wishing she had Glimmer and his comforting light, she squinted and examined the riders on the birds closest to her. Clad in black that blended with the shadowy sky, they stared straight ahead, but she couldn't make out their features. They were the size of her captor, so they were most likely pixies. The riders' own wings lay motionless against their backs, allowing the birds' powerful strokes to carry them to their destination.

Zinnia's followers? Iris had said Ping would be a threat to Zinnia's rule. If the pixies knew about an heir to the throne, they might fight Zinnia. But would they rally behind a stranger?

Ping remembered the dagger Dvalin had given her. She slid her hand to her waist and touched the sheath. Yes, there it waited with its lovely blue gemstones embedded in the hilt. At least she'd have a weapon at her side when they arrived. She could fight. The odds were overwhelming. Death loomed, but could she change her fate?

Was it heroic to die with honor, but leave everyone worse off than if you'd never lived? Or was it better to bide your time and work out a plan to save yourself?

She liked the second idea better!

Perhaps there was a third path—a way to save the kingdom without losing herself. She clung to that hope, her resolve firm. She must leave the impulsive, irresponsible Ping behind in Nadavir and become the cautious, dependable princess that Pixiandria needed.

Resolute in her new mission, Ping planned as the raven bore her onward.

CHAPTER 8

Friends to the Rescue

Frigg watched in horror as a mysterious figure riding a massive black bird snatched Ping and pulled her into the air. A helpless scream tore from Frigg's throat. "Nooooo!"

The sky swarmed with ominous birds and their dark riders. Frigg lost sight of the one whisking Ping away. The raven was big, but the rider was small—a pixie? Why were these frightful pixies attacking them? Overwhelmed and confused, she trembled. Would she ever see her friend again? She plunged her face into her hands and sobbed.

There hadn't been time to fight. The small band of Nadavir friends had brought no weapons with them to see Ping and Iris off on their journey. Frigg sat and shrugged off her tears. No time for crying now. They needed action.

Iris lay nearby, unconscious, a gash on her head.

All around, the others shook themselves and rose to their feet, dazed. Tip raised his fist, shouting at birds and pixies who'd disappeared with their prisoner. Cricall galloped away in pursuit of the birds' flight path.

Dvalin sat up, his expression confused. Frigg had witnessed his valiant struggle against the kidnappers, but the lump on his head showed the outcome.

He rushed to Namis and Birgit, who huddled together on the ground. When he determined they were shaken but uninjured, Dvalin turned to Frigg. "We'll gather a search party to go after Ping."

"I'll rally as many elves as I can," Tip vowed.

Cricall returned, looking disheartened. "I lost them, but my clan will stand by us," he assured them. He lowered his horn to heal Iris's wound.

Dvalin weighed his options. "I'll wield every ounce of influence with the Council," he said. "Ping is one of us—we cannot allow her to fall into the wrong hands."

Iris clutched her head. "She's already fallen into the wrong hands. Those had to be Zinnia's followers. They won't want Ping to reach Pixiandria. They'll probably kill her."

"No!" Frigg insisted. "We can't give up. She was alive when she left here, and we must assume she's still alive and needs rescuing."

Iris shook her head, wincing from the sudden pain. "If only I could have snuck Ping into Pixiandria. I was so careful, taking elaborate precautions to hide my journey. Yet somehow, they tracked me."

Tip said. "Now, you must sneak Frigg, Cricall, and

me into Pixiandria."

"No, you younglings can't go," Namis said. "It's too dangerous."

Dvalin's alarm clouded his features. "I agree. You're not going on this mission. Invading Pixiandria and rescuing Ping requires trained soldiers."

"Trained soldiers can't breach Pixiandria's isolation barrier," Iris said, her voice firm. "It's fortified with traps and spells. Stealth is our best option. I don't know how we'll do it, but armed dwarves, elves, and unicorns would raise alarms."

Dvalin persisted. "Fine, no army. But I'll go with Iris."

Frigg stepped forward and rested her hand on her father's arm. "Da, you need to stay here to govern Nadavir. This is your place."

"But--" Dvalin began.

Tip chimed in. "If we go, Iris can lead us in as ambassadors from Nadavir and friends of the long-lost princess. We'll say that she was escorted to Pixiandria ahead of us."

Cricall cried, "Yes! Let her kidnappers explain their way out of that if they've harmed Ping."

"At least the pixies will know she was alive when she left Nadavir!" Frigg added.

Iris perched on Dvalin's shoulder. "Pixies suspect outsiders. But they'll be excited about a long-lost princess. If Ping's alive, they might welcome the friends who sheltered her all these years. If she's not, they'll want to investigate. It's a better plan."

"No, it's too dangerous," Dvalin said.

"Well," Tip said, "it was also dangerous traveling to Anasgar, but we took care of each other."

"I've been working with Dagny at the school on my defensive skills," Frigg added.

Cricall nodded. "The older unicorns are training me in combat and diplomacy. They admired my journey to Anasgar."

"We're much better at defending ourselves now than we were when we fought off the trolls," Tip said.

Dvalin sighed. "I see I'm not winning this battle."

"I can't believe you're even considering sending children on such a dangerous mission!" Namis argued.

Iris crossed her arms, her face defiant. "They may be children, but they're also the ones who know Ping best. They should be the ones to go."

Dvalin shook his head. "Let's retreat to the safety of our hearth and discuss our next move. We can't do anything until morning."

"We have to act now! Every second we waste, Ping gets farther away from us," Tip urged.

"I hate to be the voice of reason," Frigg said. "But it's too dark to find our way and we're exhausted."

Cricall nodded. "Frigg's right. We need to rest and plan."

With heavy hearts, they moved inside the mountain. Frigg turned back one last time and sent a plea into the darkness. I promise we'll come for you, Ping. Don't give up hope!

After a restless night, Frigg, Tip, Cricall, and Iris gathered and prepared to set off on their quest to rescue Ping. Dvalin, his eyes crinkling with both pride and concern, hugged Frigg and presented her with a bundle—a larger version of the one he'd given Ping. "Oh," she exclaimed, when she saw the gorgeous dagger with the red gemstone-studded handle. She gripped it, feeling its weight, and thrust it into the air. "It's beautiful!"

Dvalin's gaze lingered on her. "May the fates be with you, my precious daughter. Give Ping our love."

"To all of you," he continued, "may the runes guide your steps and may your progress be swift."

Tip extended his hand, and Dvalin clasped it firmly. Cricall received a gentle pat on the neck. Iris fluttered to Dvalin's cheek and gave it a playful poke. "I won't let anything happen to them," she declared, her wings a purple blur.

Namis handed out provisions for their packs. Unable to sleep, she and Birgit had stayed awake all night, baking honeycakes for the journey. She embraced each of them in a hug loaded with love and sorrow. She whispered to Frigg, "Be safe, my darling. Find Ping and bring her back to us."

Tears glistened in Frigg's eyes. She turned to Iris and said, "Okay, I think we're ready. How do we get to Pixiandria?

Outside the Nadavir cave entrance, Iris surveyed the landscape. "It looks different from the ground," she mused. "The doves know the way. It's hard to get my bearings with all these trees."

Tip scratched his head. "I'll climb a tree. Join me at the top, and we'll figure it out."

"Worth a try," Iris said with a shrug.

Cricall kneeled. "Hop on, old buddy."

Tip scrambled onto Cricall's back and leaped to the lowest limb of the towering oak. He climbed to the top and surveyed their surroundings, squinting against the sun.

Iris flew to his side, her wings catching the light. "I think it's that way," she said, pointing westward.

"But there's a giant ocean in that direction," Tip chewed on his lip. "How will we cross it?"

"Don't have a clue," she admitted. "The doves fly over it."

They rejoined the others on the ground.

"Did you see Pixiandria?" Cricall asked.

Tip said, "Nope, but it looks like we'll have to cross an ocean to get there."

Cricall groaned. "How do you cross an ocean?"

Iris said, "I've seen boats gliding on the water. Maybe we could get one of those."

"Even if we find a boat, how will we move it?" Frigg asked. "I can't steer a boat."

Tip grinned. "You sail it! I have experience sailing boats. Lakes, rivers, you name it—I've navigated them. Remember the mysterious breathing cave on our way to Anasgar?"

"Yes," Frigg said. "Lakes are much smaller than oceans."

"What is an ocean, anyway?" Cricall asked.

Frigg sank onto a nearby log. "It's like a colossal lake, but crossing it'll take days, perhaps weeks."

Tip added, "And let's not forget the hazards—enormous waves, sea monsters, storms, and the dreaded seasickness."

Iris couldn't help but giggle. "You're painting quite a dramatic picture. I've observed countless ships sailing across the ocean. Surely, it's not as bad as all that?"

Frigg said, "It's probably even worse. Are you positive we have to cross the ocean? Is there another way to get to Pixiandria?"

Iris said, "No, I'm afraid not. I fly across the ocean every time I come to check on Ping. You can't go around an ocean."

"Well, I guess we need to get ourselves a boat." Tip thought a moment. "Could you shift into one, Frigg?"

Frigg sighed. "A boat big enough to sail across an ocean is enormous. I don't think I could manage becoming something that huge. Turning into a troll was stretching my skin to capacity."

"Okay," Cricall said. "We must go where there are boats. Then we need to find someone who knows how to steer one across an ocean. That shouldn't be too hard."

"A harbor," Tip said. "That's what we need."

"Yes, but there's a bigger problem," Frigg said. "If we find a harbor, there'll be humans—people who might not readily welcome a dwarf, an elf, and a unicorn aboard their vessel for an ocean voyage."

Tip added, "We'll probably need money to pay our way."

Frigg smiled. "Da gave me gemstones. I don't know if we have enough to buy our way."

Tip said, "I've read sea stories of people working on boats to pay for their passage."

"How could we work on a boat?" Cricall asked.

"I could climb the ropes," Tip said. "Not sure what they do after they've climbed them, but my climbing skills are top-notch!"

Cricall's head drooped. "I'd have to hold a rope in my teeth. Can't climb with these hooves."

"No, but perhaps they need your strength or healing skills." She paused. "I've also read stories about stowaways. They sneak onto the boat and hide down below."

Tip said, "If they're caught, the captain makes them walk a wooden board jutting over the water, and they plunge in."

Iris gasped. "That sounds dreadful!"

Cricall's voice rumbled. "I've no desire to jump into the water! I don't know if I can swim."

"Me neither," Frigg said. "Let's not stowaway if we can help it. All this talk isn't getting us onto a boat and across that ocean." Frigg turned to Iris. "Do you know where we might find a harbor?"

Iris's wings fluttered with excitement. "I think I know just the place."

CHAPTER 9

Dragonflies Don't Do Subtle

Over the next two days, Iris soared above the friends as they made their way through the forest and up a winding hill. It proved a grueling climb, scrambling over rocks and helping Cricall find a path through. But each difficult breath reminded them of their shared mission to find Ping. At last, they reached the summit. Before them lay a vast expanse of water, stretching like a shimmering blue blanket to the distant horizon.

"Does it go on forever?" Cricall asked with amazement.

Iris tilted her head, her purple wings glistening in the light. "No, not forever. There's land across the water."

"How far?" Frigg asked.

"I've never actually measured."

Tip pressed. "How long did it take you to fly over it?"

"My doves were tired after crossing, but they weren't exhausted."

Frigg grinned with relief. "Now that's helpful information. Perhaps this isn't an ocean. Maybe it's a channel or a giant lake."

"We still can't walk across it," Cricall said. "We'll need to find a boat. Where is this harbor?"

"It's around that cove," Iris pointed to a small circular area sheltered from the waves. "We can walk down to the beach and skirt around that dune. The harbor town is on the other side."

"A town?" Frigg asked with a frown.

Tip said, "I read in those sea stories that harbors and towns go together. Sailors need places to eat, unload their boats, and replace those crew members who fell off the boat during their journey."

"Fell off the boat?" Cricall's eyes widened.

"Oh yes, people fall overboard all the time. They don't get their sea legs and are wobbly," Tip said confidently.

Iris added, her wings aflutter. "I've watched it happen as I fly over. They slip and slide all over the deck, and then plop, right into the water they go." Iris's smile seemed a bit too cheerful for the topic.

"Will I slip and slide?" Cricall fidgeted. "Smooth surfaces and rocking decks aren't my specialty."

Tip considered the problem. "We might tie you to something with rope."

Frigg patted Cricall's neck. "We'll think of something. Surely, they take horses on boats all the time. You're like a majestic horse. We'll ask the boat's captain what we should do to keep you safe."

Cricall shifted uncomfortably.

Tip said, "Wish we had some pickular sap that helped us stick to the bridge on our way to Anasgar. It would stick to the ship deck."

Frigg and Cricall exchanged knowing glances. The sap had indeed saved them from plummeting off the rocky bridge across Banaga Canyon.

The hike down the hill was much easier than the climb up had been. Following a dirt path that led to the beach, they watched the sun sinking into the water as they approached the rocky shoreline.

At the bottom, Tip voiced the next concern. "Won't the captain ask where we're headed?"

Frigg halted, realization dawning. "I hadn't considered that," she admitted. "We need the name of a destination. But telling the captain we're bound for Pixiandria might not be sensible. Iris, any ideas?"

Iris, her expression perplexed, flitted closer. "No, I head for a tree with the doves. I don't know the tree's name."

Frigg chewed on her bottom lip, her mind racing through options. "Maybe we can find a map or ask somebody when we get to the town. But our first concern? How will humans react when a dwarf, elf, & unicorn stroll into their town?"

Tip said, "I'll go in alone. I can pull my hat low over my ears—might pass as a short human."

Cricall asked. "Are there short humans? The only one I've ever seen was the tall lady who captured Frigg."

"Sam." With a nose wrinkle, Frigg made her dislike clear.

"Yes, Sam," Cricall agreed. "Frigg is probably too short and there's no way I can hide my horn. I've never heard of a tiny, flying human, so Iris is out."

"I can take the shape of a hummingbird, butterfly, or dragonfly," Iris revealed casually. "I do dragonfly best. It's the wings, you know!"

"You can shape-shift?" Frigg asked, surprised.

"Only those three forms," Iris said. "We learn early to disguise ourselves. Some pixies can mimic bees, moths, even flies. But dragonflies suit me. Never needed anything else."

Frigg's mind whirred. "I can shift, too. I'll take Sam's appearance since I know what she looks and sounds like. Iris can flutter along as a dragonfly. Cricall, we'll arrange a boat and figure out how to get you onto it."

"Perfect," Tip said. "A brilliant plan!"

"Not sure about brilliant, but it's a plan," Frigg chuckled.

Cricall surveyed the area. "I'm not thrilled about being left behind," he admitted. "But I'll stick out in the town." He looked around the beach. "I need a hiding spot."

They scoured their surroundings until they discovered a shallow cave. With a bit of brush to conceal it, the cave would remain unseen from both the beach and the cliff—a sanctuary for Cricall. He trotted inside and wished them luck.

Tip pulled his cap over his ears.

Frigg focused her mind, conjuring an image of Sam,

the human who had captured her during their daring quest for Anasgar. She pictured the tall, thin body wearing a blue-checkered shirt and dirty trousers, her dark, stringy hair drooping to her shoulders. A haggard face with fleshy bags below her eyes peered out under a brown, wide-brimmed hat. With a determined effort, Frigg shifted, expanding and molding into Sam's image.

She cleared her throat and attempted to imitate Sam's low, gravelly voice. It took a few tries to get the raspy gruffness just right, but soon she shuddered to hear that dreadful voice coming from her own throat.

"How did you make your clothes look dirty?" Tip marveled, eyeing Frigg's transformation.

"Sam's clothes were always grubby," Frigg explained. "Guess that's how I imagined them."

Iris wrinkled her nose. "Not very pretty," she declared, her own transformation underway. In a shimmer of colors, she became a beautiful green and purple dragonfly, wings glinting in the morning sun.

Frigg stared, impressed. "Wow! You're beautiful!"

Iris waggled her dragonfly tail. "Thank you," she said, twirling in circles, the iridescent colors of her body sparkling in the morning sun. "Dragonflies are naturally flashy!"

"Uh," Tip said. "Do you think you might be a bit too flashy? I mean, we want to blend in and not draw attention."

Iris huffed. "Dragonflies don't do subtle."

Frigg said, "You are stunning, Iris, but Tip's right. Can you tone it down a bit—especially while we're in the town?"

"I'll try," Iris said. Slowly, a duller green and a light lavender replaced the iridescent colors. "How's this?"

Tip opened his mouth to speak, but Frigg beat him to it. "Perfect," she said. "Thank you, Iris."

With their disguises in place, the trio examined each other for flaws. Satisfied, they set off toward the harbor town.

CHAPTER 10

Finding a Boat

When Frigg and Tip stepped into the town of Portside, they gawked at the unfamiliar sights and sounds of a bustling human harbor town. Finding the docks was a breeze—they looked up and followed the towering masts of the boats, which loomed like giants in the mist above the water. For a mountain-raised girl like Frigg, these boats were like colossal creatures capable of devouring entire caverns.

A drizzly dampness filled the air, and soon the rain soaked their clothes. Frigg offered Iris a cozy shelter in her pocket to shield her delicate wings from the wet. Humans of every shape and size hurried about them. Sam's old clothing proved perfect for the docks. Frigg saw many checked flannel shirts of faded red, blue, and green.

As the fog slowly lifted, rays of sunlight pierced the gloom, revealing the town's narrow streets lined with quaint shops. The weathered storefronts boasted names that tickled Frigg's curiosity—Olsen's Saloon, Betterson's Dry Goods, Ed's Grocery. She pondered the existence of dry goods. Did a wet goods store exist? What mysteries might a grocery or saloon reveal? The aroma of freshly baked bread from Betty's Bakery made Frigg's stomach growl.

The sound of church bells and the squawking of seagulls carried out to the water, and the taste of sea salt lingered on Frigg's tongue.

"Where should we go first?" Tip's voice plucked her from her thoughts.

Frigg shrugged. "Should we pick a boat and ask for the captain?"

"Sounds like a decent idea."

As they approached the nearest vessel, its immense size stunned them. Sailors hustled around it, hauling cargo onto the deck. A winch creaked, clinking metal against metal, as it lifted a crate of unknown goods. Frigg gathered her courage and approached a sailor who was tugging a hefty rope. He ignored her and continued working.

"Excuse me, kind sir," Frigg ventured with a smile, but the sailor was lost in his own world of ropes and sails. She tried again in a gravelly Sam voice, "Pardon, sir."

The sailor, a gruff old seafarer, barely glanced her way as he barked, "Away with ye. I'm busy."

Frigg pressed on. "Yes, sir, I see that, but could you direct us to the captain of this fine boat?" The boat seemed dilapidated and creaky, rather than fine, but she thought it best not to mention its faults.

He paused, giving them the once-over, then grunted without letting go of the rope, "Oi, Bill, help this lady, will ye?" And with that, he resumed his struggle with the rope.

Bill, a burly fellow with a beard as dark as the ocean's depths, lumbered over. "What's your pleasure?" he growled.

"We're in search of this noble vessel's captain," Frigg repeated. "Can you help us?"

Squinting, he appraised them with a sailor's keen gaze. "Aye, I might. What do you want with the captain?"

Tip jumped in, "We're looking for a reliable boat to travel across the ocean."

"The ocean? You mean the channel here?" Bill asked, a hint of amusement in his tone.

"Yes," Frigg said, "we seek passage across the channel."

Bill eyed their humble garb. "Got coin?"

Frigg puffed up, pride in her stance. "Indeed, we're prepared to strike a fair bargain."

"Hah! Not sure about a fair bargain, but captain takes on a few passengers now and again. Won't set sail for a spell. He's not here today. Come back tomorrow."

"Are there other boats ready to travel? Today perhaps?"

"Hmm, probably not today." Bill scratched his beard. "*Neptune* might be nearing departure."

"Many thanks," Frigg said, but Bill had already

turned and rushed away.

As they moved along the dock, Iris darted ahead, returning with an eager nod. She looped joyously above their heads, reminding Frigg of Ping's vivacious spirit. They trailed Iris to a sturdier boat, where sailors loaded wooden crates.

They caught a sailor's attention. He grumbled, "Harbormaster books passage."

"Where's the harbormaster?" Frigg asked.

"Town," he muttered, then he hurried off.

Tip observed, "Sailors have little time for pleasant-ries, it seems."

"Guess we'll ask in town."

The first person they asked pointed to a wooden sign reading *Harbormaster*. It swayed over a well-worn door.

Frigg exchanged a nervous glance with Tip, and they approached the building. "Here we go." She turned to Iris. "You'd better get in my pocket or wait out here. I'm not sure if dragonflies go inside buildings."

"Gives me time to explore a bit," Iris said.

Tip pushed the door open and gave Frigg an encouraging nod as they stepped uneasily into the dim building interior. The darkness intensified when he shut the door, but with their years living in caves, their eyes adjusted quickly to the shadowy room.

Two humans engaged in a heated discussion at a counter with a man sporting long sideburns. He shook his head. "Nothin' headed to Northumber in the next few days. The closest you'll get is Amsterville."

The lady wrung her gloved hands. "But Amsterville

is fifty miles from Northumber."

Her companion shrugged. "We'll have to hire a coach."

"But the cost!"

"Can't be helped," he said. "Only way to get there." He turned back to the man behind the counter. "What's going to Amsterville?"

The man consulted the paper in front of him. "*Neptune* sails tomorrow."

"We'll need two tickets." He reached into his pocket and pulled out some paper. "How much?"

As the humans completed their transaction, Frigg whispered to Tip, "He's got some kind of paper currency."

"We've got your da's gems. Let's barter like we do at the Nadavir market."

Frigg spotted a map hanging on the wall. "Hey Tip, check this out!" Frigg leaned in, her mind flickering through memories of Ainsel's endless geography lessons. The territory was unfamiliar, yet the symbols had a cozy familiarity reminiscent of those used by dwarves. "This star is where we are," Frigg pointed to Portside on the map. Her gaze followed the jagged line where land met sea, the Hyberg Channel. "That must be the channel the sailor mentioned."

Tip's finger glided across the map to Amsterville. "That's where *Neptune* is going. Guess it's as good a place as any to get across."

They continued to study the map until the couple finished their transaction and moved away from the counter. They took deep breaths and approached with all the confidence they could muster. Tip asked, "Sir, when might we set sail for Amsterville?"

The Harbormaster's brows rose like a pair of seagulls taking flight. "Amsterville? Right popular place today."

"Is that so? I hear it's lovely. Do you have a boat leaving for it soon?" Frigg asked.

"Yes, we have a ship on the morrow." A smirk played on his lips. "They're ships. Boats are tiny ducks compared to these giant swans."

"Ah, of course, a ship," Tip said with a nod. "Tomorrow, you say?"

"Yep," confirmed the Harbormaster, his gaze piercing, as if he could see through Tip's cap to the elfin ears beneath.

Frigg jumped in, "How long is the journey?"

"A day, maybe two, wind permitting. Two tickets you'll be needing?"

"Yes, plus one horse," Frigg added quickly.

"So, add a crated horse in the cargo hold. That'll be an extra charge," the man said as he wrote some figures on a paper. "Total cost is forty-five eups."

Frigg did not know how many gemstones forty-five eups equaled. She fingered the smallest gem in her pocket. From the shape, she thought it was a ruby. She pulled it out. "Will this be enough to cover the cost? It's all I have."

As soon as the man saw the ruby, his eyes bulged with greed.

Frigg instantly knew she'd made a mistake. The ruby was way too valuable for their fare, but it couldn't be helped.

"That'll do," he said, snatching the ruby. "Livestock crate will be ready at *Neptune's* berth. Pier 16, three ships down on your right. Here are your documents. Be there with your steed at dawn."

Tip took the papers and let out his breath. "Thank you," he said to the man.

They left before the man demanded more.

Once outside, Frigg whispered, "How will we get Cricall into that crate without everyone seeing his horn?"

"We'll think of something," Tip assured her. "We always do."

Iris fluttered down to Frigg's shoulder.

Frigg said, "That's settled then. We'll be sailing for Amsterville at sunrise. We need to collect our horse and load him into a crate."

They strolled toward *Neptune*, its towering presence promising their next adventure. Sailors loaded crates into a large hole in the ship's deck.

"Hope they have room for Cricall after loading those crates," Tip said. "They've got a mountain of them."

Frigg wrapped her arms around her body, shivering in the brisk wind. "I hope Cricall won't mind riding for two days in the belly of a ship. It's probably dark and cold down there."

Iris darted above the commotion, her keen eyes scanning the shadowy depths of the hold. She zipped back with the news. "It's black as a raven inside. Not a fun place to spend any time."

Tip scratched his head. "I don't see any other way to

get him onto that ship."

Frigg let out a long sigh. "Let's head back to the beach and talk to Cricall. We'll let him decide whether he wants to ride in the cargo hold."

She sent an anxious plea into the air and hoped it would reach Ping. *We're coming for you, Ping! Stay strong and stay safe!*

CHAPTER 11

Loading a Unicorn Isn't Easy

As the sun peeked over the horizon early the next morning, Frigg and Tip led Cricall through the cobblestone streets of Portside. A large burlap sack covered Cricall's head, hiding his eyes and the magical healing horn that spiraled from his forehead.

Never once in their discussion with him the night before had Cricall wavered in his will to go onto the ship, despite the hardship he'd encounter stuck below deck in the ship's dark belly. Frigg and Tip had promised to check on him often.

The burlap sack idea to hide Cricall's horn had come to Frigg when she was unpacking supplies from the sack. If anyone asked, they'd say Cricall's skittish around ships, and we're keeping him calm by not permitting him to see what's happening. They'd assure the busybody that he'd be fine once in the ship's hold.

Iris tucked herself in the outer pocket of Frigg's rucksack.

For Frigg and Tip, the voyage ahead called for a sprinkle of magic and a dash of disguise. Frigg had never held an illusion for this long and hoped for a hidden nook on the ship where she could return to her true self, if only for a moment. Tip had to keep his cap pulled over his pointed ears.

Neptune's seasoned sailors eyed Cricall's burlap sack with a mix of suspicion and wonder as he bravely stepped into the giant crate waiting on the pier. The sailors worked with hammers and ropes, and soon the crate soared high. Frigg and Tip anxiously watched as the crate swayed over the ship's deck, but the sailors expertly maneuvered it into the hold.

They scurried up the gangplank to the ship, where a surly captain stood. He glanced at them, examined their papers, and then motioned to his right with a grunt. They found their cabin with help from a sailor who asked if he should go into the hold and take their horse's sack from his head.

"No," Frigg blurted. "He'll stay calmer with it on. We'll go down as soon as the ship sails. Get him settled and fed."

"Okay then, we want the boy to feel safe. That was a nifty trick with the sack. I'll remember it for future jumpy horses."

Once the ship sailed, the rolling waltz of the waves tested Frigg's resolve to visit Cricall. Her legs could not find their sea rhythm and an upset stomach resulted.

In the cabin's seclusion, Iris, now a pixie once again, offered words of comfort. However, her soothing skills were as wobbly as Frigg's sea legs. "We'll be there before you know it," she said. "You'll feel much better on the shore. Until then, buck up. Tell yourself not to be sick. It'll pass in no time."

Frigg didn't feel like bucking up. She felt like puking and that's exactly what she did, luckily over the side of the ship. She made it clear to Tip that she didn't want anyone to pat her back to soothe her. His stomach immune to the channel's sway, Tip took the hint and devoted his time to Cricall.

Tip told Frigg that his secret nearly slipped away with his hat when he fell asleep and woke to hear voices in the hold with him. He shook the sleep from his head and realized his hat had come off just as two sailors rounded a crate and almost fell over him.

"I recovered my hat right quick!" Tip said. "But it was a close call."

Holding Sam's form was easy for Frigg, but her mind was dizzy from seasickness. Occasionally, her body would revert to its original Frigg self before she made it to her quarters. The nice sailor had supplied her with a bucket to keep in the cabin in case she couldn't make it to the deck. Whenever she fell ill, the odor would drive her out of the small cabin to empty the bucket. Twice she forgot to transform into Sam before leaving the cabin.

Iris frequently vanished. Sharing the cramped cabin with a queasy dwarf proved no place for a pixie. Frigg didn't blame her for longing to fly free in the fresh air.

Finally, they reached the other shore and the town of Amsterville. When they came ashore, Frigg and Tip had one goal: to whisk Cricall away without drawing curious eyes. The plan was unfolding perfectly. With a groan and a creak, the crane hoisted Cricall's crate from the hold and positioned it on the dock with a thud that echoed through the morning's brisk air. A sailor clambered atop and pried out the nails.

Tip stepped forward to lead Cricall from the crate. A curious onlooker peered over his wire-rimmed glasses, his gaze fixed on Cricall's shimmering coat. "What a magnificent sheen! It's like gazing through a crystal. Pray tell, what breed is this radiant horse?"

"Uh-h-h," Tip stammered, caught like a deer in lantern light. "I-it's a white one."

"Indeed, but what kind of white one?" pressed another gentleman, his mustache bristling with curiosity. "I've never seen it's like."

Frigg moved to Cricall's side and summoned a voice of authority. "He's a lumigrand, a rare breed from the East."

"Ah," the first man said, eyes sparkling with interest. "I'm a horse trader, you see, and a lumigrand is new to me! I'd sure love to see more. Remove that sack so I can get a good look. I might make you a generous offer."

"He's not for sale," Tip said, steering Cricall away from the man.

But the mustached man was quick, reaching for the burlap. It clung stubbornly to Cricall's horn, but with a few tugs, it came loose.

"Stop!" Frigg's voice rang out, but it was too late.

As the sack fell away, gasps rippled through the spectators. A hush fell over them as Cricall blinked in the sunlight, his horn glistening.

Finally, someone in the crowd broke the silence. "It's a unicorn," she said in a hushed voice.

The crowd buzzed with astonishment. "Unicorn?" "Incredible!" "Can it be?"

Frigg acted swiftly. "No, no, it's not a unicorn. There's no such thing. Lumigrands are bred to resemble unicorns." As she spoke, she grabbed Tip's arm and walked him backward, away from the crowd. His hand was on Cricall's rope, so Cricall slowly followed them.

"But he's the spitting image of a unicorn," insisted the bushy-mustache man.

"It's all for show, designed to dazzle and delight. That's where this one's headed now, the Exhibition of Freakish, Abnormal, and Bizarre Creatures.

"A freak show?" a woman said. "Well, I never."

The crowd seemed too stunned to stop them, parting like the sea, allowing them to retreat.

Reaching the crowd's edge, Tip jumped onto Cricall's back, pulling Frigg up behind him. Tip jogged the rope. "Galloping garnets, Cric, go fast!"

Cricall surged into a sprint, his hooves drumming a rapid beat. As he ran, Tip's hat flew off.

Shouting came from behind them. "An elf! Halt!"

The angry shouts of people chasing them continued to the town's edge. But Cricall was swift, and he didn't stop until they'd reached safety deep in the surrounding woods. They listened and welcomed the silence.

"We're clear," Frigg confirmed, peering back.

"That was a narrow escape," Tip said. "I wonder why they were so angry."

"Perhaps because we tricked them?" Frigg suggested.

Cricall's breaths came in rapid, rhythmic bursts after his wild ride, his sides heaving with each breath and his nostrils flaring wide. Finally, his breathing slowed to normal. "I'm just glad to get off the ship and out of that crate. Freedom is wonderful!"

Frigg opened her pack. "It's safe to come out, Iris. Any idea where we go from here?"

Iris soared from the pocket and shot into the air. "I'll check the view from above to find a landmark."

She flew higher and soon was out of sight.

CHAPTER 12

The Princess Arrives

Ping's eyes snapped open, her heart fluttering like a trapped butterfly as she experienced the peculiar sensation of tumbling through the air. Blinking away sleep, she realized it wasn't her cozy bed she was clinging to, but the warm, feathery back of a majestic bird.

The raven's wings sliced the air as it spiraled gracefully downward. A heavy layer of clouds below hid their destination. Ping shut her eyes tight, trying to quell the dizziness bubbling inside her. Riding atop such a magnificent creature was a far cry from the freedom of her own wings. Her stomach pitched, and her head grew hazy.

When she dared to peek again, a towering stone spire loomed ahead, its top crowned with an arched window. The bird glided through the opening and circled the room, coming to rest on a raised wooden platform.

Her captor released the grip that had been holding her in place during their flight. He stretched with a slight groan and dismounted. He was an older male with a closely trimmed beard. His hazel eyes twinkled with mirth as he reached for Ping.

She brushed aside his outstretched hand, her pride as ruffled as her wings. With a determined flutter, she tried to take flight, but her stiff limbs and wings betrayed her, resulting in a rather ungraceful plopping to the ground.

The pixie's chuckle was light and friendly. "A helping hand can soften the landing, Princess."

With a huff, Ping relented. "Fine, help me to my feet."

"Nothing would please me more," the pixie replied, his voice as smooth as spiderweb's silk. "I am Lord Sycamore, at your humble service." He bowed and tipped one wing to the ground, offering his hand once more. This time, Ping took it, finding her balance with his support.

Lord Sycamore guided her down to the floor beneath the platform. A pixie boy approached. His hair strands were intertwined with prickly sticks, green leaves, and small red berries. "Father, everything is prepared," he announced with a respectful tip of his orange and white wings.

Sycamore acknowledged his son with a nod, and the boy turned, bowing deeper to Ping, his smile bright and cheerful. "Welcome to Pixiandria, Princess. Your arrival fills us with joy!"

Ping stared. She wasn't filled with joy. But she now knew where she was.

The boy continued. "I'm Hawthorn, but please call me Thorn. I'm certain we'll become best friends!" He handed her a flower brimming with golden nectar.

Ping eyed the drink suspiciously. Were they trying to poison her? What would that accomplish? A missing queen and a dead princess. Well, that would take care of the royal succession. But they could have killed her in Nadavir and been done with it.

She found herself thirsty and accepted the flower, sipping the syrupy nectar. When it didn't immediately kill her, she gulped noisily. It tasted like honey and soothed her parched throat.

"Thank you," she said, passing the empty flower back to Thorn.

Much refreshed, Ping turned to Sycamore and snapped, "Why did you kidnap me?"

Lord Sycamore's smile was gentle. "Would you have come, if I'd asked?"

Ping met his gaze. "I was on my way to Pixiandria with my Aunt Iris when you flung me onto your giant black bird. I am not impressed, nor will I forget your actions."

"Princess, I only hoped to ensure your safe arrival. And here you are! Your aunt could not have guaranteed untroubled entrance to our land."

Ping snorted and surveyed the enormous room filled with huge ravens and their pixie riders. "Where are we?"

"Pixiandria Palace's east tower," Lord Sycamore replied, his voice filled with a hint of pride.

"Pixiandria Palace?" Ping repeated.

"Naturally. Where else would I bring the heir to the crown?"

Ping tilted her head, a lock of hair turning a curious brown. "You still haven't explained why I'm here."

"Ah, Princess," Lord Sycamore began, "our beloved Queen Aster has disappeared. Until she returns, the realm requires someone of royal blood to grace the throne. As her daughter, that someone is you."

Thorn's head bobbed. "Yes! Queen Aster would be so proud."

Upon receiving a glare from Sycamore, Thorn's shoulders hunched, and he ducked his head.

Ping's lips formed a tight, thin line. "What if I don't want to be a princess?"

Lord Sycamore chuckled. "Being a princess isn't something you choose; it's who you are."

Ping frowned. "But I didn't do anything to earn it."

"That's the way succession works. You were born into the royal family; therefore, you are a royal. You'll become the ruler when your mother steps down or dies."

Ping bit her lip. "And if I refuse?"

"Surely, you are not serious." Lord Sycamore's cool expression slipped a bit. "Your royal obligation is to rule over the land. It is the natural order of things."

Ping stood firm. "Not in Nadavir. They don't have a queen of dwarves. They have a council. The people elect their leaders. Well, the men used to decide, but since Frigg saved everyone from the trolls, not only Frigg, others were there, including me, but the fact is now women vote and are on the Nadavir Council."

Thorn, who had been listening intently, chimed in. "That sounds like our Kaboodle!"

"Kaboodle?" Ping asked, curious.

Thorn nodded eagerly. "The Kaboodle advises the queen, but she makes the ultimate decisions."

Ping said, "I don't want to make ultimate decisions. I've lived happily without knowing I was a princess. Find someone else to do it. Your kidnapping of me has changed my mind about wanting to come to Pixiandria. I want to go home. Let's climb back on that bird and return me to Nadavir."

"I'm afraid that's not possible right now," Lord Sycamore said. "The ravens need rest. Stay with us tonight. In the morning, we'll talk more. After you tour the palace and meet with the Kaboodle, you might see things differently."

Thorn bounced on his toes. "Yes, please give us a chance to introduce you to Pixiandria. I promise it's a magical place."

Ping considered this, too tired to argue anymore. She was curious about Pixiandria, despite her strong words.

"Okay, one night. But then I'll go home if I don't want to stay longer." She paused. "I wish I could meet my mother. Does anyone know what happened to her?"

Regret shadowed Sycamore's face. "She vanished without a trace, I'm afraid."

Ping observed the pixies in their dark attire tending to their birds, her mind racing. "Did Zinnia order you to kidnap me?"

Sycamore met her gaze with surprise. "Zinnia? No, she didn't command us. She wanted to extend an invitation, to ensure you'd take the crown rightfully. I was simply tasked with ensuring your safe journey."

"But Iris said..."

"As I mentioned before, Iris couldn't protect you. The guards and I could."

Ping's thoughts tumbled like leaves in the wind. Iris had painted Lady Zinnia as a villain, but here was Lord Sycamore, suggesting she was concerned for Ping's safety. If Zinnia wasn't after the throne, then what happened to the Queen? Iris had suspected dark deeds, but now Ping wondered who was friend or foe? After all, Lord Sycamore had abducted her!

"I hope Queen Aster returns before I leave, but I have to get back. I have important things to do in Nadavir. Being the only faery in the colony is an enormous responsibility."

Lord Sycamore smiled. "I am sure it is. We'll return you if you decide you need to go. But I hope you will give the Pixiandria faeries a chance to get to know you. We've been waiting to do so for a long time. You might discover you like it here."

Ping felt a flutter of uncertainty. She searched Sycamore's expression for answers, but it revealed nothing, as unreadable as a closed book. Thorn's beaming face displayed an open book of hospitality.

"Perhaps some rest and a spot of refreshment would do you good," Sycamore suggested kindly. "Let's get you settled in your chamber, and we can sort everything out in the morning. Is that agreeable?"

Ping nodded, her eyelids heavy with fatigue. "Yes, please. I'm too tired to think."

Sycamore turned to his son. "Hawthorn, fly ahead and inform Violetta of our arrival. I'll accompany the Princess to her quarters."

"Yes, Father." With a leap and a flutter, Thorn zipped away like a shooting star.

Sycamore turned back to Ping. "Do you feel like flying, or would you prefer to walk?"

"I think walking is preferable until my wings have time to fluff. They got a bit squished during the ride here." She gave him a reproachful scowl.

"My deepest apologies, Princess. Long journeys are not without discomforts," he said, his voice tinged with regret.

"Humph," Ping replied

CHAPTER 13

Pixiandria Palace

Sycamore led Ping through an arched doorway and into a passage illuminated by floating orbs of light. Ping delighted in the walls adorned with green vines blooming with vivid pink flowers that emitted a soft, otherworldly glow.

Her exhaustion melted away as she experienced the surrounding wonders. The polished crystal floor felt cool on her bare feet and its transparency reflected a tapestry of colors cascading from the stained glass windows.

Ping turned her hair orange with happiness and then included a few blissful pink strands.

Unlike the stone furniture the Nadavir dwarves favored, faeries seemed to like delicate, pixie-sized furnishings. Sofas and chairs crafted from twisted branches and decorated with flower-petal pillows rested in cozy nooks high in the walls. It dawned on Ping that flying faeries could gather to chat there.

The caverns of Nadavir were massive compared to the gallery where a fountain of sparkling water murmured a soothing melody and featured tiny sprites dancing on its surface. To a pixie, this hall was both enormous and elegant. A troll's head would have touched the ceiling.

Sycamore said, "The palace lives within an ancient oak tree."

"We're inside a living tree?"

He laughed. "Yes, astounding, isn't it?"

"And quite magical," Ping whispered, her eyes wide with amazement.

They ascended a spiral staircase wrapped around a huge oak column. "Embedded in this pillar are leaf-bound books. They contain our faery wisdom. Watch this." He plucked a book from the wood and another book with the same title grew slowly in its place.

The air in the palace was fragrant with the scent of jasmine and lavender. "This is the evening scent, a boon to restful sleep."

"How lovely," Ping said.

"I'm sure you'll find it pleasurable. In the morning, peppermint with a hint of eucalyptus encourages refreshing wakefulness. The afternoon scents are citrus and rose hips to assist with alert concentration."

Ping thought about Nadavir, where the bodily odors of many magical folk living in a giant enclosed space mingled.

The palace's grandeur overwhelmed Ping, despite its small-scale features. Her feet were growing tired, and she fluttered her wings to see if they had recovered enough to carry her. She floated upward and Sycamore joined her.

They rose to the top level, where Sycamore stopped in front of a door intricately carved with images of faeries in flight and round flowers with massive petals. "Those are peonies," Sycamore said when he saw her examining the blooms. "Your mother had them included for you."

"They're beautiful," Ping replied. "I've never seen flowers like those before."

Sycamore raised an eyebrow and pushed open the door, revealing a delightful space that shimmered with enchantment. Blues and lavenders whirled across the space. A luxurious four-poster bed, draped in a velvety moss blanket, invited her to sink into its silken pillows.

Ping guessed it was ten times the size of her modest bed in Nadavir. Dvalin had made the Ping-sized bed for her. Birgit had created adorable mini bedding and pillows for her. Functional and comfortable, it was familiar and overflowing with love.

A female pixie with kind, curious eyes flew across the chamber, tipping her wings as she curtsied in mid-air.

"Hello," Ping said.

The pixie dipped into another curtsy. "Your Majesty, I am Violetta, your attendant. It will be my honor to help you settle into life in Pixiandria."

Ping smiled. "Thank you, Violetta. I appreciate any help you can offer."

Sycamore flung open curtains, revealing a wall of

closets. Ping floated, openmouthed in astonishment. Dresses in a kaleidoscope of colors hung suspended from branches. Each one was a masterpiece of artistry.

"Are all these for me?" Ping's voice was filled with disbelief and delight.

"Yes, Princess. If there's a particular dress you desire, your seamstresses would love to craft it for you."

"My seamstresses?"

Sycamore nodded. "Indeed. You have many at your command."

Ping stood amidst a sea of garments, each more splendid than the last. She had always worn the same trusty blue dress, which, by some enchantment, never bore a single smudge or wrinkle.

They moved to a corner table overflowing with a treasure trove of treats. Fruits of every hue and shape were piled high—some familiar, others mysterious and begging to be tasted. A pot of vegetable stew sent up steam curls, while a crystal goblet sparkled with a drink that caught the light like a gemstone. Beside it, a teapot promised secrets of spices and herbs.

With a flourish of his hand, Sycamore presented the feast. "We've prepared a banquet fit for a princess." He looked to Violetta, who added, "Not knowing your favorites, we made an assortment of foods to choose from."

Ping whispered a stunned, "Oh," as words eluded her.

Sycamore chuckled. "I hope you find everything agreeable, Princess. Should you have a need, Violetta can take care of it."

Ping's gaze traveled around the chamber, taking in the splendor that nurtured pixie comfort. Something stirred in her heart, a feeling as new and wonderful as the dawn.

"I'll leave you to rest and refresh. We have much to discuss tomorrow." Sycamore bowed again and closed the door behind him.

"Your Majesty, is there anything I can help you with?" Violetta asked.

"No, thank you, Violetta. I think anything a pixie could want is right here."

"When you have eaten, I can help you dress for bed."

"That won't be necessary. I'm used to taking care of myself. You can go. After all this work, you must be tired."

Violetta's eyebrows raised. "Your Majesty, I couldn't..."

"Yes, you could. I'll see you in the morning," Ping said firmly.

With a puzzled expression on her face, Violetta curtsied and left.

Once alone, Ping twirled, arms outstretched. She took flight, her laughter echoing as she explored her new surroundings. Eventually, she landed on a plush chair at the table, sampling the spread before her. Each bite was an adventure, though her stomach fluttered with a storm of emotions.

She sipped tea from a teacup as delicate as a seashell, enjoying the pungent aroma and taste. It was a far cry from the humble acorn cap she used at home.

The sparkling drink from the crystal goblet soothed her from within. When she had her fill and the whirl-wind inside her calmed, she leaned back and pondered her origins, her family in Nadavir, and the worry they must feel in her absence.

The tales Iris and Sycamore told offered very different stories about what was going on in Pixiandria. Who was she to believe? Who could she trust?

In that quiet moment, with her only companion the moon's silver glow through the window, the weight of her situation struck her. She'd never felt so important, yet also so helpless. She allowed the tears to come, a silent river carrying her fears and hopes alike.

CHAPTER 14

Royal Dawn Delicacies

As Ping's eyes fluttered open, a sense of bewilderment washed over her. Gone was the familiar cozy comfort offered by her tiny bed nestled in her Nadavir room. She wasn't clutching the feathers on the back of a raven, either.

Instead, she found herself enveloped in an opulent sea of satin, a pillow so luxurious it seemed to swallow her whole. With every wiggle and squirm, Ping sank deeper, like being caught in a marshmallow trap!

But Ping was not one to surrender.

Determined to escape the bed, she lay on her tummy, wings spread wide, and with a few strategic flaps, propelled herself backward. It worked, and she finally broke free from the satiny snare. She rose into the sunlit chamber.

Hovering above the bed, memories of yesterday's events came into sharp focus. Zinnia! Was she a villain, as Iris said? Or had she sent Lord Sycamore to retrieve Ping and place her on the throne? Today, she resolved to uncover the truth.

Ping glided to the door, her ears perked for any sound. A curious latch high on the door caught her attention. How odd! Why would you latch the top of a door? Then the answer dawned on her—this was a realm where fairies soared more often than they strolled. Such fairy-friendly conveniences were still new to her.

She peered into the silent hallway—no guards in sight. This wasn't a prison then. The unlocked door offered proof of that. She glanced at her jeweled dagger lying untouched on the nightstand where she'd placed it last night before sleeping. Sycamore hadn't taken it away from her or even acted like he'd noticed it. Perhaps there was a sliver of truth in his words.

With a swift motion, Ping flew to the nightstand and snatched the dagger, securing it at her side. Until she knew who to trust, it'd be her constant companion. She whisked through the doorway, easing it shut. There was no need to announce her freedom.

Wishing for a map, she resolved to seek places to conceal herself and eavesdrop on conversations. Dwarves were prone to revealing secrets when they believed themselves alone—fairies were likely the same.

She descended the grand, spiraling staircase. At the bottom, drawn by the clink of dishes and hushed voices, she moved to an open doorway. There she hovered, listening intently.

"How do we know she's a real princess?" a doubtful female voice asked.

"Lord Sycamore brought her back, didn't he?" another female said. "He must be sure."

"Well, I don't know about you, but I'm not tipping my wings to a stranger," declared a third voice.

"I'm with you, Petal. We can't just accept her as the new queen without proof."

"Where's she been all this time?"

"Maybe she's an imposter!"

Ping's hands balled into fists. An imposter? The very thought! How she yearned to reveal herself and dispel their doubts! But what if they were correct? What proof did she have that she was the princess?

The voices drifted away. Ping flew through an arched opening, straight into a dining hall grander than any she'd seen. Miniature tables filled the hall, each draped with an embroidered tablecloth that seemed to have captured joys of nature—vibrant flowers, playful butterflies, and darting hummingbirds. The tables were low and surrounded not by chairs but by vibrantly colored cushions.

Upon the tables rested dishes crafted from the finest polished wood, their surfaces gleaming. Sparkling crystal glasses caught the light, scattering rainbows across the hall. Were they setting the table for breakfast? She was used to more simple mornings with Frigg, grabbing a quick bite or a bowl of Birgit's hearty porridge. They gathered at the big dining table only when Dvalin was home and insisted they dine as "proper young ladies."

A twinge of worry seized Ping. Would her simple dwarf manners be out of place for this fancy faery setting?

"Are you hungry?" The sudden question, gentle yet unexpected, made Ping jump. She spun around to find Violetta hovering behind her.

"Yes, I hoped to find tea and perhaps a biscuit," Ping said with a smile.

Violetta curtsied, her wings tipping forward. "Certainly, Princess. It's too early for the others to arrive for Dawn Delicacies. They tend to sleep in quite late. Please have a seat at the head table, and I'll fetch some tea. Do you prefer flower or herb?"

"Flower tea sounds delicious, thank you," As the girl turned to flutter away, Ping said, "Violetta, you don't have to call me Your Majesty. Please call me Ping."

Violetta froze. "Oh, Your Majesty, that wouldn't be proper." She turned and zipped away.

Ping sighed softly to herself. "Making friends might be a challenge if everyone insists on Your Majestying me. But I definitely think I'm going to need some friends."

Ping fluttered to a table across the hall. Positioned apart but facing the other tables, she guessed this was the one Violetta had meant. She plopped onto a bright red cushion and waited for her tea.

A wooden stick sporting several pointed spikes lay in front of her, next to a spoon made with a petal-shaped hollow, and a dagger with a serrated edge. They fit perfectly in her petite hand, a delightful novelty from eating with her fingers in Nadavir because the dwarfs' chunky utensils were too large for her to hold. Birgit always made sure small wood pieces were beside her plate. The dwarves used the pieces to pick food from their teeth. Ping used them to stab hot food, so she didn't burn her fingers.

Violetta glided into the hall, a tray with a silver teapot floating behind her. Without spilling a drop, it descended gently onto a hot pad made from woven vines—no magic words, no faery dust, only the silent wonder of enchantment.

Ping's heart skipped a beat. "Faery magic! Violetta, how did you do that?" she cried.

Violetta paused with surprise. "Pardon me, Your Majesty?"

"The floating tray! Did you use faery dust?"

"Faery dust?" Violetta echoed, her brow furrowing.

Ping slowed her words, hoping to make herself clear. "Do you possess a special magic that causes the tray to float so gracefully?"

Violetta's eyes widened in realization. "Yes, Your Majesty. But surely, you wield such magic?"

Ping hesitated, a flicker of uncertainty crossing her face. "I...I'm not sure I have magic."

A moment of silence passed before Violetta responded, her voice gentle and reassuring. "You must be gifted with magic, Your Majesty. You are a pixie, after all."

"Perhaps." Ping's mind raced with possibilities.

Violetta's expression brightened. "I believe you should meet with The Ancient One. She's a sage with great wisdom. I'm sure she can help you find your magic. Shall I arrange a visit?"

Ping pictured Hilla, the wise Nadavir oracle. The seer's penetrating gaze often made her uneasy, because Hilla had a way of making Ping think she was peering directly into Ping's soul. But Hilla's wisdom was as deep as her kindness. "Oh, yes, Violetta, that would be wonderful!"

As Violetta poured the tea, the doorway became a parade of floating trays, each filled with delectable treats—cakes as light as air, puddings smooth as silk, fruits glistening like jewels, and pies promising sweetness in every bite.

Ping cried, "Such a feast! I couldn't possibly eat everything!"

Violetta reassured her with a smile. "Fear not, Your Majesty. We weren't sure what you liked for your Dawn Delicacies, so we prepared several dishes. Please taste those that interest you and let me know your preferences."

"Dawn Delicacies?"

"Yes, we have three main meals in the palace: Dawn Delicacies, Noon Nibbles, and Moonlight Morsels. We serve them in this grand hall, but I can bring a selection to your chamber if you prefer."

Ping's Dawn Delicacies progressed with dishes floating past her. She savored each, her expressions of joy or polite rejection observed by Violetta.

The faery cuisine flavors were unlike anything Ping had known, each tidbit a symphony of elegant sweetness, in stark contrast to the nourishing but simple dwarf meals. Between bites, she drank a little tea or juice, eager for the next delightful surprise. Soon, she pushed a dish aside, her gaze lingering with dismay on the untouched delicacies hovering nearby.

"My, oh my, I'm absolutely stuffed!" Ping declared, her hands gently patting her round tummy as her hair blossomed into a brilliant tangerine color.

Ping wondered why Violetta looked confused and was about to ask, when Violetta said, "That's fine, Your Majesty. We can continue tomorrow. I have an idea as to your tastes now and will make sure your menus are to your liking."

She cast a thoughtful glance at Ping's blue dress, the same dress she had arrived in the day before. "Would Your Majesty fancy a change into something from your wardrobe? I can assist you and style your hair."

Ping considered the idea. "This dress is my one and only. A swift shake to free it from dust, and it's as good as new. And my hair? A quick tousle with my fingers and a frolic beneath the waterfall does the trick."

Observing Violetta's valiant effort to conceal her surprise, Ping wondered if tales of her messy ways would flutter about the palace. She didn't know Violetta well, but there was no hope for it if her confidences were repeated. Violetta was her best chance of learning about life in Pixiandria.

Violetta said, "I suggest we return to your chamber and discuss your options."

Ping agreed readily. She had to be presentable when she met the others.

Once back in Ping's sunlit chamber, Violetta guided her to the cozy nook by the window. Ping could gaze upon the castle's enchanting gardens while Violetta tended to her locks with gentle strokes, weaving magic into every twist and turn.

The previous evening's arrival on the raven's back had been cloaked in darkness, and Ping hadn't seen the palace grounds. Now, with the morning light spilling through the glass, she marveled at the splendor of the gardens unfurling below her.

The kingdom was stirring to life. The courtyard's meandering paths were aflutter with flying fairies, their wings shimmering in the sun. Some hovered over blossoms, basking in their sweet scents and vibrant hues. Birds chirped merrily, flitting amongst the petals, while insects hummed their daybreak songs.

"Does it meet your royal approval, Your Majesty?" Violetta inquired with a hopeful twinkle in her eye.

So absorbed was Ping in the garden's charm she hadn't noticed Violetta's finishing touches. She snapped back to the present and gazed into the mirror. Who was this stranger staring at her? She didn't recognize the face in the mirror as her own. Soft pink curls framed her face with delicate tendrils cascading from a sparkling tiara centered on her head.

"It's amazing!" Ping cried. "Thank you, thank you, thank you!"

Violetta's cheeks flushed with pride. "I'm glad you like it, Your Majesty. It pleases me to see you happy."

As they spoke, Ping's hair shimmered, shifting into a procession of colors that left Violetta awestruck.

"Your Majesty, your hair changes color!"

Ping nodded, a smile playing on her lips. "Of course,

doesn't yours do that?"

Violetta shook her head. "I noticed it in the grand hall but thought it was the light."

"My hair has always changed with my moods. I thought it was faery magic."

"It might be," Violetta said. "But I've never witnessed such a marvel before. Some pixies can alter their wing colors, their sparkles, or their hair sprigs."

"Sparkles? Hair sprigs? I'm not sure what that means."

"You'll notice some pixies radiate a shimmering light called sparkles, akin to twinkling stars. When we're young, flowers and leaves sprout in our hair to match our names—flower petals grace the girls, tree leaves for the boys. We call them hair sprigs." Violetta pointed to the violets entwined in her curls.

"How extraordinary! My hair has always responded to my feelings, changing by itself. I've been able to guide its shades as I've grown. Faery Rule #5: Don't question the colors."

Violetta's eyes sparkled with curiosity. "Faery Rules?"

Ping laughed. "They're my own creations. In Nadavir, the dwarf colony where I grew up, there were no other faeries to teach me, so I made my own rules for being a faery. I've penned eighteen so far."

Violetta's face lit up. "So imaginative! I'd be honored to learn them. It'd help me serve you better. We have unwritten rules, but nothing so formal."

Ping grinned. "They're not formal decrees, but they are my truths."

Encouraged by Violetta, Ping selected a gown from the gigantic closet—a lavender frock featuring a billowy-sleeved blouse and a skirt that floated gently around her legs. Hidden shorts beneath the skirt ensured modesty, and as she moved, a subtle floral fragrance enveloped her, as if the gardens themselves had blessed her new attire.

Violetta explained, "Each gown is infused with the essence of a different bloom or spice, from the gentlest rose to the boldest cinnamon. They're designed to echo your feelings, guiding you to a dress which harmonizes with your heart's mood for the day."

Ping's eyes glistened with delight. "Absolutely magical!" she exclaimed, her hair blossoming into a radiant pink.

"Your Majesty, may I pose a question?" Violetta ventured with a hopeful smile.

Ping giggled. "I think you just did."

"Yes, I guess I did, but may I ask another?"

"Absolutely."

"Why have you not ventured to Pixiandria before now?"

Ping thought for a long time before answering.

Violetta blushed. "Forgive me if I've been too bold. You needn't answer."

"No, it's not that. I'm simply searching for the words to explain," Ping assured her. "Until yesterday, I didn't know there was a Pixiandria to come to. I knew nothing of this realm—not of my mother, nor of her royal lineage. I wasn't even aware I was a princess."

Violetta gazed at her, empathy in her eyes. "You

must have felt very alone."

"Not really. I was raised among dwarves with my dearest friend, Frigg. I've been happy and loved. But something was always missing. I guess that something was Pixiandria."

Tinkling bells gently signaled the passage of time.

"Ah, we must go. I set a reminder so we wouldn't be late," Violetta said, her voice tinged with excitement.

Ping shook off her memories. "OK, lead the way. I'm eager to meet The Ancient One."

CHAPTER 15

The Ancient One

Ping trailed behind Violetta, weaving through the palace's endless corridors. She tried to memorize their path, but the many twists and turns made her dizzy.

Pixies hurried through the corridors but moved aside, tipping their wings, when they recognized their princess. Ping smiled and nodded, fascinated by their sparkles and hair sprigs. After her talk with Violetta, she resolved to learn about the trees and flowers of Pixiandria so she could identify pixies' names by the petals and leaves in their hair.

Soon Violetta slowed at an archway that led to a separate wing of the palace. "That's where The Ancient One lives," she said with a giggle Ping found charming. "She awaits your arrival. I'll stay here to guide you back."

Ping would have preferred Violetta's company. But

then she remembered she was the princess and needed to embrace royal-size bravery. Her back straightened, her hair rippled into a bold blue, and she glided ahead.

The red door before her featured a unicorn-shaped knocker. It reminded her of her friend Cricall and their shared adventures. Gathering new courage from those memories, she lifted the unicorn's horn and announced her arrival with three strong taps.

For a moment, nothing happened. Then the door creaked open. Ping entered a realm of emerald enchantment. She'd stepped into a forest. The air in the chamber was heavy with an earthy scent, filling Ping's nostrils with its musky aroma. Green hues surrounded her, from the velvet moss on the walls to the leafy canopy overhead. Her fingers grazed the bark on a nearby tree. She marveled at its rough texture, the tiny ridges and grooves sending a shiver up her spine. Tiny fireflies swirled in the air, their glow casting a gentle golden light.

Was this woodland real or an illusion?

She searched for The Ancient One, but the chamber seemed empty.

A hushed silence filled the chamber, as if the very air held its breath in anticipation of The Ancient One's arrival. Ping's curiosity and excitement overflowed. "Hello?" she called into the leafiness.

A beautiful young woman in a glittering jade gown, adorned with intricate patterns, floated toward Ping. Her brilliant glow radiated an exotic grace.

Ping shielded her eyes, smiling into the brightness. "I'm Ping and I seek The Ancient One's guidance."

The light softened as the woman's gaze met Ping's. Her laughter chimed. "Pixiandria has long awaited you, Princess. I am The Ancient One, Pixiandria's sage."

Despite her youthful appearance, something about The Ancient One's gleaming green eyes suggested a lifetime of smiles. There was a slight crinkle around the edges, deep and knowing, wise and strong. Yes, this woman was older than she looked. Those eyes knew much more than they revealed at first glance.

Ping relaxed her shoulders, trying to mirror The Ancient One's grace. "Well, if you know who I am, then you know why I'm in Pixiandria. My Aunt Iris was bringing me, but fate had other plans. Lord Sycamore whisked me away against my will me on an enormous raven."

The Ancient One regarded her with a gentle head tilt, her gaze piercing yet kind. "Your arrival, though unusual, is a cause for joy. Over the years, I sensed your energy in the Great Expanse and assured your mother you were alive, although there was a moment last year when I wasn't sure." She pressed her lips into a thin line. "Your life force flickered weakly." She straightened and smiled. "You seem to be much better now."

Ping's breath hitched. Memories of the mine accident that injured her came flooding back—a time when darkness had almost claimed her. The Ancient One's ability to detect Ping's life force from afar indicated an impressive magical power.

"Yes." Ping nodded. "I was injured while far from

home. As you can see, I have recovered."

The Ancient One's eyebrows raised. "Home? Do you see Nadavir as home, or are you referring to Pixiandria? Of course, you were far from either, but Pixiandria has always been your true home."

"Nadavir is the only home I've ever known."

"Ah, I see. But we hope you will come to think of Pixiandria as your home now that destiny has guided you to our embrace."

Ping hesitated, then blurted, "As long as I'm here, can you tell me if I have magic and how to use it?"

"Magic flows through you, strong and waiting to be encouraged," The Ancient One said. "Do you realize you've been using magic to change your hair color several times since you've been here?"

"But that's not magic! It's just something I do."

"But it is magic! Your magic is mostly snoozing, but we can awaken it with effort."

Ping stared. "Are you sure?"

"Yes, work and practice unlock your power. Lack of training and knowledge held you back."

"I'd love to conjure floating food trays." Ping's mind buzzed with possibilities.

The Ancient One's laugh tinkled with amusement. "We shall achieve such an ability and more." She grew serious. "Magic holds the power to protect, for not all is light in Pixiandria. We must keep you safe."

"Keep me safe?"

"Yes, be cautious, my dear. Dark forces lurk in Pixiandria."

"Did these dark forces take my mother?"

The Ancient One's voice was tender. "The manner in which she vanished and her current whereabouts are unknown to me. Her spirit still flickers faintly, so she breathes. Yet, I feel a tremble in her life force, a sign she's not where she wishes to be."

"Like me." Ping's heart skipped. "Taken, not by choice."

"Indeed, young one. Your paths seem woven by the same mysterious thread."

Ping's resolve strengthened. "Then I must learn how to use my magic, and quickly. When do we begin?"

The Ancient One shook off her seriousness. "How about right now?"

Ping's spirit soared. "I'm ready if you are."

"Join me." The Ancient One beckoned, gesturing to a sea of cushions. Ping chose a yellow one as bright as the sun and settled upon it, shifting her hair to an eager orange. The Ancient One sat opposite Ping on a forest green cushion.

"Close your eyes," The Ancient One instructed, "and let your mind drift to a place that fills you with joy and peace. Perhaps a favorite spot."

Ping thought about her little bed alcove in Nadavir. She liked to sit on the bed and chat with Glimmer or Frigg and write in her rule book. She pictured herself on her bed and wished she were there.

"Are you in that relaxing place?" The Ancient One inquired.

"Yes," Ping whispered.

"Now, let an object from that place occupy your

thoughts. Focus on every detail.

Frigg's blue marble hairbrush materialized in Ping's mind, its bristles a forest where strands of her golden hair had tangled. Oh, how Ping missed being tickled by those hairs while sitting on Frigg's shoulder!

"Focus on the object," The Ancient One urged. "Hold your thoughts steady. Don't let them flutter away."

Ping's thoughts returned to the hairbrush, which was far too heavy for her to lift. She furrowed her brows to concentrate even more. The blue color was her favorite. It almost matched her blue dress. A dress she realized she was no longer wearing. She had changed into this lavender dress earlier. What a sensation! It felt a little strange, this new dress. Her old one had molded to her skin because she had worn it for so long.

"Concentrate!" The Ancient One repeated. "Your mind is all over the place. Keep returning it to the object."

Ping refocused on the hairbrush. Hairbrush, hairbrush, hairbrush. Repeating the word in her mind helped.

"Now, imagine the object rising. Just a little at first."

"Do I need a spell? Like magic words or something?"

"No, we generally have no need for incantations except for ancient spells or those of major importance."

Bursting with determination, Ping pictured the hairbrush rising.

"Maintain your focus," The Ancient One encouraged. "Let it rise slightly and hold it there with the strength of your magic."

Ping's magic wrapped around the hairbrush, but the brush stubbornly stayed put. Rise, silly hairbrush. It shot into the air.

"Just a smidge," The Ancient One guided. "Imagine it floating, as light as a feather on the breeze. Don't let it fly away!"

The hairbrush dropped onto the dresser. Ping tried again. Focus, focus, focus. Hairbrush rise.

To her amazement, the hairbrush lifted a few inches and hovered.

The Ancient One encouraged her. "Don't let it drop. You are in control."

"I did it!" The hairbrush dropped to the dresser, but Ping's eyes sparkled with triumph. "I really did it!"

The Ancient One beamed. "Indeed, you did."

"Was it only in my imagination? It didn't actually rise in Nadavir, did it?" Ping thought about what a surprise that would be for Frigg, watching her hairbrush floating.

"Your magic is not yet strong enough to reach across lands, so no, it didn't physically rise in Nadavir. But one day—"

A sudden knock interrupted their moment.

The Ancient One's smile faded. "Enter," she called with a hint of reluctance.

Lord Sycamore strode into the chamber, bowing with tipped wings. "My apologies for the intrusion. I'm here to escort the Princess to the Kaboodle meeting."

"Kaboodle meeting?" Ping asked.

"Yes, Princess, the Kaboodle seeks your audience to discuss your mother's disappearance."

Ping perked up. "Perhaps they have some answers."

Lord Sycamore bowed again. "I will be at your side to assist you."

"Peachy," Ping said with a smirk. "I'm always ready for an adventure."

She turned toward The Ancient One. "Thank you for the lesson. I can't wait to try again. May I return?"

"Anytime, Your Majesty. I'm at your service. Our journey of discovery has just begun."

Ping took flight with Lord Sycamore, ready to unravel mysteries with the Pixiandria Kaboodle.

CHAPTER 16

Meeting the Kaboodle

Outside The Ancient One's quarters, Ping bid farewell to Violetta, who promised, "I'm only a thought away. Shout my name in your mind, and I'll be by your side."

"Well, that's quite handy for me," Ping said. "But what about Rule #3? A faery does what she wants, when she wants."

Surprise flashed across Violetta's face, then she grinned. "I'll always want to assist you."

Their laughter mingled for a moment, a shared secret.

"I'll try not to take advantage of your kindness," Ping replied.

Both Lord Sycamore and Violetta seemed stunned by her answer.

"It's not mere kindness," Violetta said. "It's my sworn duty to serve my princess."

Ping's hair turned an embarrassed purple. "I'd prefer not to have that burden. I'll be careful not to call you too often. Ping Rule #7: Faeries won't be a nuisance to people they like."

Lord Sycamore harrumphed as he led Ping away.

"Slow down!" Ping called after him. "I've got questions before we meet the Kaboodle."

Sycamore paused and turned, a picture of patience. "Ask away, Princess. What would you like to know?"

"What is the Kaboodle like?" Ping asked.

"The Kaboodle consists of nine advisors and Queen Aster," Lord Sycamore explained. "We represent the regions of Pixiandria and gather monthly to discuss issues. Queen Aster considers our suggestions before making decisions."

"What does she have to decide?"

"Everything relating to Pixiandria. The Queen's role is important, her power immense."

"Great, and you want me to wield that same power in her absence?"

"You won't have to do it alone. The Kaboodle will guide you, sharing our seasoned wisdom and experience."

Ping recalled the Nadavir Council's tedious debates about things Ping thought trivial. Frigg loved council meetings and listened intently until the end. Ping often dozed in her friend's pocket. Staying awake during a dull Kaboodle meeting would be a challenge.

"What happens to Pixiandria if I leave, and my mother doesn't return?"

Lord Sycamore's expression darkened. "Chaos

would ensue. Without a royal family, ambitious pixies would fight for control. Zinnia might be the Kaboodle's choice, but others would contest her rule, risking conflict, even war."

"What about Aunt Iris? She's Mom's sister. Couldn't she rule?"

The horrified look on Lord Sycamore's face told Ping the answer before he said it. "Oh, no! Iris as queen? She's not in the line of succession. Your mother became a queen through marriage. She and King Rowan ruled the kingdom equally, and when the King died, Queen Aster had the right to rule under pixie law. But her sister is a royal only because she's related to the Queen. She cannot take the throne."

"If the Kaboodle can appoint Zinnia, why can't they appoint Iris?"

"Iris lacks the necessary qualities to rule." He hesitated. "And her concentration is often scattered."

Ping nodded. "Yeah, I guess she doesn't have strong focusing skills." Ping considered her own difficulty picturing the hairbrush, but thought she probably shouldn't mention it.

Lord Sycamore harrumphed.

Ping contemplated a kingdom with Iris in control, where bewilderment replaced harmony. It wasn't a promising picture.

"Alrighty, then," Ping announced with a spark of adventure in her voice. "Lead the way. Let's meet this Kaboodle and be done with it." She braced herself for the difficult encounter ahead.

Lord Sycamore, with a flourish of his wings, said,

"As you wish, Princess. The Kaboodle meeting chamber is this way. But before we go, may I offer some advice?"

Ping bristled. She was tiring of his advice, but she nodded anyway.

"As I said earlier, Kaboodle members are wise and will assist you in running Pixiandria."

Ping prepared herself for more predictable instruction, but Lord Sycamore's words took an unexpected turn.

"They may perceive you as an outsider, perhaps questioning your youth and experience. It's important for you to let them know you are in charge. You must take control right away. It's crucial to plant your roots swiftly and show them your sturdy branches. You haven't the luxury of time to blossom slowly. Your mother, a mighty oak in her own right, commands the forest with her presence. You must unfurl your leaves and show the Kaboodle you are the seedling of her legacy."

Ping wasn't sure how she'd show them her sturdy branches or how to unfurl her leaves. Did she have branches and leaves? What did it all mean? How could she rise to such a towering task? How could she take control? A memory sparked her thoughts—a moment of defiance in the Anasgar Council Chamber when she and Frigg stood before the Council, their plea for aid against the trolls initially cast aside. Her own fiery, faery spirit eventually swayed them to join the fray.

Now was the time for that same spirit to blaze forth.

They navigated the corridor maze until they reached a grand door, its wood intricately carved with tales of ancient times, of pixies fighting enormous beasts. With a nod from Lord Sycamore, the door swung open, revealing the Kaboodle's inner sanctum.

Sparkling chandeliers cast a brilliant glow on the elegant paintings that adorned the walls. Inside, eight pixies lounged on fluffy cushions, a feast of fruits and sweets spread before them. They paid no attention to Lord Sycamore and Ping, eating as they noisily chatted and laughed.

One pixie sat with regal poise on the grandest cushion, a figure of authority, her gaze sharp and commanding. She silently watched everyone, but did not take part in the chaos surrounding her. Her long black hair, crowned by a sparkling tiara, flowed around her shoulders. Ping guessed from her demeanor that this was Lady Zinnia, the one who coveted her mother's throne, a force to be reckoned with.

Taking a deep breath as she'd seen Frigg do before confronting someone, Ping steeled herself for the encounter ahead.

Silence cascaded through the room, heavy with anticipation, as the Kaboodle members noticed their princess. They remained seated, their eyes appraising her with curiosity and skepticism.

Zinnia's smile was a mask of pleasantries. Behind that smile, Ping sensed a hidden storm brewing. "Ah, our cherished princess graces us with her presence. Forgive me, your name eludes me—how forgetful. What was it?"

Ping realized this was her moment to assert herself, but she didn't have the slightest idea how to do that.

She drew inspiration from her memories of bravery observed in the past and floated forward. Her gaze slowly met each Kaboodle member's eyes, her heart beating in a rhythm of courage and resolve. Their mouths opened in surprise as she changed her hair to a vibrant royal blue, straightened her shoulders, and in a clear, steady voice declared, "It is a supreme honor to meet the esteemed members of my mother's Kaboodle."

A murmur rippled through the room, but Ping's spirit did not waver. "I am Princess Ping, daughter of Queen Aster and King Rowan, heir to the throne of this wondrous land." She locked eyes with Lady Zinnia. "And you are?"

Lady Zinnia's smile stiffened along with her posture, her eyes fixed on Ping's determined gaze. A silent battle of wills played out between them. "I am Lady Zinnia, the appointed steward of Pixiandria in the Queen's absence. Your return is a joyous event for us all," she said, her voice dripping with both sweetness and underlying tension.

Ping's fiery faery spirit blazed within her. "I stand before the Kaboodle, ready to find my mother and embrace my destiny."

The Kaboodle members were stunned by her bold proclamation, their expressions filled with surprise and intrigue.

But Ping refused to be underestimated or pushed aside. She trembled inside, but if she needed to be here to lead, that is what she'd do. She didn't dare glance at Lord Sycamore. What must he be thinking?

The room fell into a respectful hush. Then, as if prompted by an unseen force, the Kaboodle members rose one by one, each offering a wing-tip salute and bowing their heads in acknowledgment of Ping's authority. Unsure of the proper etiquette, Ping simply floated before them and tried to look royal.

The last one to stand and tip her wing was Zinnia. She did not bow her head, and the smile did not leave her. Ping searched for a hint of emotion—anger, amusement, respect? It was hard to tell. Ping wished Zinnia had the same talent as she did for her hair color broadcasting her emotions.

Zinnia spoke. "We welcome you, Princess Ping. We are so glad you've come during this trying time. Would you like to join us?" Zinnia gestured to an empty cushion.

Ignoring the offered seat, Ping flew to the larger cushion once occupied by Zinnia. "Is this my mother's place?" she asked.

Zinnia nodded, her eyes betraying a flicker of surprise.

"Then I shall sit here. It will make me feel closer to her during this trying time."

Zinnia moved aside. She glided to the empty cushion she had originally offered to Ping, her wings leaving a shimmering dust trail behind her.

After claiming her rightful place in the Kaboodle, Ping searched the members' faces for a clue about their involvement in her mother's disappearance. Did any of them know where her mother was? How would she ever find out what happened?

"We'll dispense with introductions. You can share

your name as you speak. Now, my mother's disappearance. Who oversees the search? What is being done to locate her?"

"I am Lord Evergreen, the Guardian of Protection," a man with the wings of a fly and a complexion resembling tree bark said. "We have everyone out searching for her."

"Who is everyone, and where are they searching?" Ping inquired.

"We have our palace guards and volunteer forces scouring every nook and cranny of Pixiandria, every home searched, every tree examined, every path explored."

"Sounds widespread. Do we know what might have happened on the day she disappeared?"

"Alas, after ending our meeting that day, Queen Aster retreated to her chamber to dress for Noon Nibbles, but never graced the table," Lord Evergreen recounted.

"Thank you, Guardian of Protection. Hopefully, we'll have news soon. Please prepare a detailed report explaining everything you've done and all you plan to do to find Queen Aster."

She pictured Dvalin standing before the Nadavir Council with his giant rock gavel. She imagined a Ping-sized gavel and proclaimed, "Now, what matters require the Kaboodle's wisdom?"

Lady Zinnia said, "Fear not, young sovereign. We have everything under control. Surely, you wish to acquaint yourself with the palace's wonders. This must all be strange for you."

Ping nodded. "Yes, everything is very different. But

we have important matters, and I can learn about Pixiandria as we go. What is next on the schedule?"

"Forgive the interruption, Your Majesty. I'm Lord Chestnut, the Guardian of Time," another member said. His mosquito-like wings fluttered as rapidly as his eyes blinked. His ridiculous purple suit that was far too small for him brought laughter to the back of Ping's throat, but she swallowed it down. "You see, we finished our business, and we were on the cusp of adjournment when you arrived."

Ping sighed. "I'm sorry to keep you longer, but you'd better go over the business you have conducted and let me decide whether I agree. Where shall we start?"

A sea of puzzled faces met her announcement.

A faery with a round, cherubic face, her cheeks displaying a rosy hue betraying her nervousness, tipped her dragonfly wings, "Princess Ping, I'm Lady Tulip, Guardian of Orderliness, at your service. I've taken the notes at the meeting. I'll be happy to update you."

"Lady Tulip, I'm pleased to meet you! I'd greatly appreciate your review."

The Guardian of Orderliness revisited the day's discussions and explained the business of running Pixiandria. Over the next two hours, Ping and the members of the Kaboodle explained each item on the agenda.

If she had no clue what they were talking about, Ping agreed. But she felt she needed to show some leadership, so she disagreed occasionally and asked that guardian to write a report. It pained her to realize she'd have to read a mountain of reports. But, if that was the price to save Pixiandria for her mother, she'd pay it.

CHAPTER 17

A Friendly Idea

After the Kaboodle meeting ended and Ping had enjoyed a delightful Noon Nibbles in her chamber, Violetta whisked her away on a tour through the palace. With a twinkle in her eye, Violetta revealed hidden passageways and cozy hidey-holes, divulging secrets known only to those who worked in the castle.

Ping remembered Lord Sycamore had mentioned the palace dwelt within a large oak tree. Now, she discovered the palace had been planted as a seedling within the young oak tree's trunk many centuries ago and had grown with the tree over the years.

Why did oak trees seem familiar? Faery triads! Ping remembered reading about faery triads, areas where oak and two other trees stood branch to branch, creating portals into faery realms. Ash was one, and birch? No, hawthorn, that was it! And Hawthorn was Thorn's name!

Despite Violetta's marvelous tour, the Kaboodle meeting had unsettled her. With each new Pixiandria discovery, a small voice within her whispered, "This isn't where I belong." She longed for the familiar Nadavir tunnels. Although her Noon Nibbles had satisfied her with wonderful aromas and delicious tastes, she yearned for a bite of Birgit's scrumptious honeycakes.

A persistent question tugged at the edge of her mind. Why had her mother sent her away? Iris had said it was to keep her safe, but how much simpler this would be if she'd grown up in Pixiandria. She'd have the knowledge to navigate this world, to find her mother.

But if she'd grown up here, she'd never have known Frigg or Tip or Cricall. She wanted to return to them, to be surrounded by friends.

Lord Sycamore always seemed to be too busy to discuss returning her to Nadavir. She'd stayed for her day and met the Kaboodle as promised. She'd made a show of strength as he'd asked. Now, she wanted to jump on a raven and return home. Or did she?

In the days that followed, Ping discovered more wonders in the palace. She adored the fact that everything was pixie sized. The furniture did not engulf her. The food was a perfect fit for her dainty mouth—no more settling for crumbs or breaking off bits. She didn't need to perch on the broad shoulders of dwarves to avoid their enormous feet or flutter in front of their faces to catch their attention.

One sunny morning, as the palace gardens bloomed with roses and magic sparkles, Ping and Thorn strolled along the pathways.

"I can't get over how tiny the flowers, birds, and insects are!" Ping said.

Confusion crossed Thorn's face. "What do you mean?"

"In the world outside Pixiandria, they are much bigger. I'm the size of a hummingbird in that world, but here, a hummingbird is tiny enough to sit on my finger."

Thorn laughed. "You must be joking."

"No, it's a much bigger world outside Pixiandria's boundaries. An enchantment must cover this realm that makes things small."

"I've never been outside Pixiandria. It must be an amazing and somewhat frightening place."

Ping smiled. "Yes, it's amazing, and you're right, a teensy bit scary sometimes."

Palace attendants lingered nearby, ever watchful.

Ping leaned in and lowered her voice. "How do you handle being constantly watched?"

Thorn's forehead furrowed. "Watched?"

Ping sighed, her orange satin gown rustling as they walked. "I'm always on display. Attendants hover like bees. I must be at my best, and everyone endlessly asks me if I need anything. It's utterly exhausting."

Thorn grinned. "But, Princess, it's part of being royalty."

Ping stopped and planted her hands on her hips, determination blazing. "Call me, Ping. Nobody ever does anymore. It's always Princess this or Your Majesty that. I miss being Ping."

"Alright, P...Ping," Thorn stammered, "if that's your desire."

They ventured beyond the manicured hedges and gilded fountains. The palace gardens gave way to meadows filled with lush grasses and wildflowers waving in the playful breeze. Ping spotted an ancient tree in the distance, its twisted branches reaching for the sky. With a mischievous twinkle in her eye and lively pink hair, she flew ahead and called back to Thorn, "Last one to that tree is a troll lover!"

"Princess—I mean, Ping! Wait!" Thorn's voice trailed behind as he soared to keep up.

"Not waiting!" she called, her laughter weaving through the golden air. She performed a loop-de-loop, her skirts billowing as wide as her iridescent butterfly wings.

Thorn chuckled. Then he looped in a clumsy whirl, the thrill of the chase lifting him higher as he followed Ping's laughter.

When Ping reached the ancient tree, she perched on the highest branch, her eyes wide as she surveyed the land. Thorn joined her, chest heaving, and collapsed on the gnarled limb.

"Guess I'm a troll lover," he gasped, wiping sweat from his brow.

Ping's gaze shifted up, watching black shapes soaring in the distance, silhouettes against the sky. Ravens bore tiny riders, their wings glinting on their backs. She turned to Thorn. "Why aren't the ravens small? Is there an enchantment to make them big?"

"Yes, they need to be big enough to carry the guards who protect Pixiandria. When regular pixies need long-range transport, they ride large doves."

Ping nodded. "Iris said that she rode doves to Nadavir." She wrinkled her nose. "What are those ravens doing?"

"They're on patrol." Thorn explained.

"Patrol?"

"Yes, they're looking for any trouble."

Ping watched as the ravens circled, stealthy and vigilant. "Trouble, yeah, they'd know trouble."

They spent the afternoon exploring the enchanting world outside the palace walls. Ping taught Thorn how to hop the boulders, returning to the start whenever he missed one. He taught her to play tag with the fish in the babbling stream, their scales sparkling as they blew bubbles that revealed their hiding spots in the shadows.

As the afternoon sun dipped low, they rested in the grass, their breaths keeping time with the gentle hum of bees and the delicate flutter of dragonflies. Ping gazed at the sky, her mind spinning like a dandelion seed caught in the breeze. And then, it happened—the seed of an idea sprouted in her imagination.

"Insects," Ping mused aloud, "they're free, aren't they? They can be themselves, with no one wondering what they're up to."

Thorn nodded, his eyes crinkling. "Indeed, Ping. Insects are small and nobody pays them much attention. Unless they're biting someone, that is."

"Yes," Ping said, "the insects, bats, and spiders in Nadavir helped to defeat the trolls by stinging and biting. What they lacked in size, they made up for in numbers."

Maybe they could help her in Pixiandria. Insects saw everything. They may not understand what they saw. But she would.

Ping jumped to her feet. "Thank you for the enjoyable day! I think I'm ready to return and face my duties."

Thorn bowed and tipped his wings. "I'm happy I could assist you!"

Once back in her chamber, Ping told Violetta she was going to rest and didn't want to be disturbed. As soon as Violetta closed the door, Ping rushed to her window and searched the skies, her eyes alight with anticipation. A merry game of chase between a fiery-red bird and its companions caught her eye. Their wings flapped and glided as they evaded one another. She closed her eyes and called to them. "Over here, by the window, do you see? I'd like to chat."

One of them drew closer, yet kept a cautious distance.

She zeroed in on that bird and concentrated as The Ancient One had instructed her. When she opened her eyes, all the birds were nowhere to be seen. Well, this was easier thought than done!

She tried again, combing the skies and whispering a plea to join her. Eventually, a bird came into view. It was as blue as Ping's Nadavir dress. This time, instead of closing her eyes, she didn't take her eyes off it.

"Come closer, my feathered friend. I'm over here in the window. I'd love to talk to you." The bird circled but remained distant. Curious and bright-eyed, it edged closer.

Ping's gaze swept the room, spying the pastries Violetta had left. She reached for one and set it on the windowsill. "Join me for a treat," she coaxed.

The promise of the sweet got the bird's attention. It swooped down to the sill, its beak meeting the pastry's flaky layers. While the bird pecked at the pastry, Ping stood perfectly still. With a satisfied chirp, the bird claimed a generous morsel and took flight. Was this a sign of trust?

With newfound confidence, Ping called to another winged visitor, repeating the same warm invitation. Soon it feasted on the pastry. She continued with more birds until the pastry was gone. She replaced it with another, and when the next bird arrived, she tried talking to it. "My name is Ping. I'd like to be your friend."

The bluebird cocked its head, considering her words. Ping shared her heart and her hopes. It flew from the window. Had it understood her? It returned with a companion. Soon, another bird joined them. It flew away and returned with a friend. Ping moved the pastries to the table. A chorus of chirps filled the air while the birds deliberated, then, united in curiosity, they fluttered to the table.

As they gathered, their thoughts wove into Ping's consciousness. And when bees and butterflies arrived,

Ping discovered she could communicate with them as well.

The afternoon progressed into a party, a jubilant celebration of conversation and connection between a princess and the creatures of the sky.

CHAPTER 18

Friends, Foes, and Spies

During Moonlight Morsels that night, Ping found herself seated next to Lord Sycamore. With his silver hair and charming smile, he exuded an air of elegance that glowed as radiant as the golden orbs floating above them. However, Ping remained cautious of that charm. His smile always seemed to hide secrets, and she had not yet forgiven him for the frightening way he brought her to Pixiandria or the way he'd been avoiding her.

As he savored a hearty bite of roasted chestnuts, his eyes peered at her over the rim of his goblet of elderflower brew. "Rumor has it, Your Majesty," he said, eyebrows arching, "that a bird took flight from your window this afternoon."

Startled, Ping forced a laugh. "Ah, yes! A tiny adventurer flew in and perched on my sill, chirping delightfully. Quite entertaining, indeed."

Lord Sycamore focused his attention on a cluster of grapes on his plate. "Even more peculiar, it seems some butterflies and bees also exited. A remarkable coincidence, wouldn't you agree?"

With a playful tilt of her head, Ping regarded him. "Most curious. Not only that someone stared at my window so intently they noticed the flying creatures, but that such trivial matters reached your ears. Are you having me watched?"

"No, Your Majesty." Lord Sycamore chuckled and pushed his plate away. "It's simply that such a parade of creatures from your chamber is a rarity and sparked idle gossip."

Ping seemed to consider this. "I see. Aren't the birds and butterflies cherished Pixiandria residents?"

"That's true, they are."

"And you advised me to acquaint myself with the land and its inhabitants, did you not?" Ping pressed on, her voice laced with innocence.

"Quite so, but–"

"Lord Sycamore, windows are a luxury unknown in Nadavir, hidden as we are within a mountain. So, I sat at the window to enjoy the fresh air and marvel at the splendid view. A bird and a few curious butterflies ventured in. We had a lovely conversation, and they left."

Lord Sycamore's voice rose in disbelief. "Conversation? With birds and butterflies?"

"Certainly," Ping insisted. "It's vital for me to engage with all inhabitants of the realm, don't you think?"

He regarded her with bewilderment. "I think you

are a most unusual pixie, Your Majesty."

"Thank you. A compliment I gladly accept." Ping beamed.

Another voice chimed in. "I'm not certain it was intended as praise, Princess."

Lord Sycamore and Ping turned to discover Lady Zinnia floating behind them, her presence unnoticed until her words cut into their conversation.

Ping forced a smile. "Lady Zinnia, so lovely to have you join us!"

"My dear Princess, your arrival has intrigued the palace. We look forward to sharing our rich culture and time-honored traditions with you." Zinnia's eyes didn't mirror the delight in her broad smile. In fact, the darkness in them sent a ripple of unease through Ping.

"And I'm eager to learn about my pixie heritage. You see, the dwarf colony I've come from is undergoing positive changes to their outdated traditions. Pixiandria, steeped in age-old roots, may find a sprinkle of fresh insight invigorating."

Zinnia tipped a graceful wing and turned to leave, her parting words a soft murmur, "Sometimes, the old ways are best left undisturbed."

With soft moonlight spilling through the window, Ping nestled into bed that night, studying a hefty book of Pixiandrian history. Unable to concentrate after such a busy day, her thoughts turned to Lady Zinnia. So many questions! Was she the wicked person Iris had described? Lord Sycamore didn't think so. She hadn't exactly been friendly to Ping, but was she responsible for Queen Aster's disappearance? Did she aspire to rule Pixiandria?

It was hard for Ping to think about Queen Aster as her mother. Ping's daily life had lacked maternal love. She had Birgit, the kindhearted housekeeper, who treated her with love.

Namis, Frigg's mother, was not around when Frigg and Ping were young. Frigg found her during their journey to Anasgar and brought her back to Nadavir. They were trying to build a relationship, but Namis's long absence made her a stranger.

Ping's curiosity about her own mother bloomed. The regal portrait hanging with silent dignity in the Kaboodle chamber showed the Queen with poise and authority, but what would she be like as a mother? What would it have been like to have grown up in this palace with her mother to guide her? Ping ached to know the tenderness of her mother's touch, the sound of her laughter, the softness of her hug.

Ping had witnessed the magic of hugs, the way Birgit and Namis squeezed Frigg with such affection and Dvalin enclosed Frigg in his sturdy dwarf arms. But a hug was a treasure Ping had never experienced. She'd shared tender moments with Frigg, like a gentle touch on the cheek or a comforting finger on her back. Ping wrapped her arms around Frigg's finger, but the vast size difference between them made a genuine hug an impossible dream.

Pixiandria was a jumble of unknowns, and Ping longed to know more about Queen Aster. The attendants and courtiers knew Aster as their queen, but who knew the heart of the woman? Aunt Iris, with a shared childhood and sisterly bond, might have answers, but she wasn't here, and Ping wasn't sure she could trust everything Iris said.

But inspiration sparked—The Ancient One! She might help Ping understand her mother. Tomorrow, she'd ask her.

Ping's mind was a whirlwind of faces—Lord Sycamore, Lady Zinnia, The Ancient One, Violetta, Thorn, Lords Evergreen and Chestnut, Lady Tulip—mingled with the recent addition of feathered friends and buzzing creatures. Would these newfound scouts remember their mission, or would their tiny memories scatter like the morning clouds?

As Ping drifted off to dreamy sleep, a soft scurrying of tiny feet on the wooden floor broke the silence, stirring her from her drowsy haze. What could it be? Was it a friendly creature or someone come to harm her?

She floated up and snapped her fingers as Violetta had taught her. The chamber erupted into a blaze of light. "Who are you?" she shouted, changing her hair to a frightened white. "What are you doing in my room?" She blinked, squinted, and peered into the corner, searching for the mysterious visitor.

A timid squeak rose from the shadows, and a small voice offered an apology. "I'm sorry, sorry, sorry, Missy Princess. I didn't mean to scare you. But goodness, you gave me quite the fright!" said a little gray mouse, gazing up at her with eyes like polished poppy seeds. A walnut shell perched on his head and a drawstring bag clung to his back.

"Oh my," Ping said, "It was just that I was drifting off to sleep and didn't know who you were. Who are you, anyway?"

The mouse bowed his head. "Please forgive my intrusion. I'm Chia, Missy Princess, at your service."

Ping lit up her face with a smile and transformed her hair to an amused orange "Please, call me Ping. Are you a messenger mouse?"

"I'm a first-class spy, Missy Ping. I can slip into places you big people can't. I overhear whispers in the dark, uncovering the palace's deepest secrets, plots, and plans."

Ping considered this. "Your talents may be just what I need."

Chia's tiny head bobbed eagerly. "Yes, yes, yes, I heard about your meeting from a spider friend. You requested they gather news. I'm here to help." He pulled a notebook and pencil from his pack. Holding the pencil ready to write, he asked, "What do you wish to discover?"

Ping admitted, "That's just it. I don't know. My mother, the Queen, has disappeared and they want me to take over until she returns. I'm not sure who to trust or what dangers lurk."

"That's a real nut to crack, Missy Ping," Chia agreed, whiskers twitching. "But don't worry, I shall investigate. I'll sniff out what people are saying."

"So helpful, Chia. What is your fee?"

"A few crumbs in the drawer there." Chia pointed his nose at the bedside stand. "I'll check every day."

"Yes, Chia, that would be terrific!"

With a plan in place, Chia promised to return with reports from his creature network, a secret alliance of palace critters. "Spiders, ants, mice, and rats work for me."

Ping's heart swelled with hope. Perhaps she'd find allies within these walls. "Great! I'll look forward to your report."

"Wonderful!" Chia skittered off, slipping through a tiny gap in the wall. He stuck his head back through the gap. "It was excellent to meet a princess as nice as you, Missy Ping!"

Ping giggled. "And it was exceptional to meet a professional spy like you, Mister Chia!" She settled back into her bed's embrace, her worries somewhat eased. Tonight, she vowed to dream of friendships yet to bloom.

The first light of morning crept across the sky as Ping sat at her window, watching a fiery-red bird twirl around a tree in a merry game of tag with its companions. The joyful scene reminded her of a cherished memory when she and her friends took their first steps outside Nadavir's mountain on their journey to Anasgar. In the dazzling sun, birds were like dancers in the sky, and they'd invited her to join their aerial ballet. Perhaps one day she could join the local birds' dance without sparking gossip among the other pixies.

Ping turned to the table where Violetta had delivered breakfast. She crumbled a pastry, tucking titbits into the bedstand's drawer as an offering for Chia's informants. She arranged the rest on a plate and placed this feast on the windowsill, along with a cup of sweet nectar. Then she waited, smiling at the thought of giving Lord Sycamore's spies something to gossip about.

A familiar bluebird led the parade to her window, followed by a flutter of butterflies, a buzz of bees, a procession of ladybugs, and a lone, darting dragonfly. They feasted on the treats, and afterword they perched upon Ping's table, eager to share the tales they'd gathered.

An aproned lady harvested herbs from the garden with a young man who had heard Lord Sycamore was going to ask Lady Zinnia to marry him. The older lady grumbled at the extra work a wedding would create.

Children playing in the lane buzzed with anticipation of Ping's coronation, dreaming of sweets and festivities.

On a garden bench, men reminisced about King Rowan's reign, when life didn't bring about any turmoil or uncertainty.

The bees hummed, all in a tizzy over a woman who muttered about humans plotting to breach Pixiandria's magical defenses.

"Thank you!" Ping exclaimed. "Your news is fascinating. Please keep your ears open and return tomorrow!"

They promised they would. "We're overjoyed to be heard and to be your friends," added a bluebird, before they fluttered away to gather more news.

So much gossip! It dismayed Ping to face the daunting task of sifting through the chatter, figuring out aglow with pixie dust, stood to one side. Ping gently clasped her necklace pendant, a miniature vial of pixie dust scraped from colored rocks in Nadavir. The memory made her smile.

"Even though pixie dust isn't used much anymore, our wands being more efficient and less messy, your mother likes to keep that vase filled with magic as a keepsake," Daffodil shared. "I see you have a small jar of your own?"

"Yes, I keep it to remember Nadavir, where I grew up."

She touched each object on the desk. Perhaps she'd feel some trace of her mother's presence transfer to her fingertips. She opened the top book on the stack and flipped through the pages. A slip of paper fluttered out and settled on the plush carpet. She picked it up, frowning as she read the words, "Unguarded, Unprotected, Undefended, I expose you."

She held out the paper. "Is this my mother's handwriting?"

Daffodil smiled as she glanced at it. "Fluttering fireflies! Yes, the Queen's hand wrote it. True elegance in every stroke. Queen Aster always had beautiful penmanship."

"Do you know what it means?"

"A soldier's rallying cry, perhaps?" Daffodil's gaze drifted to the book. "Or a line borrowed from the pages."

Ping eyes sparkled with intrigue as they settled on the title Mysteries of the Ancient Pyxie Realm. A book about mysteries! Though the exact page from which the note had emerged also remained a mystery, she found a chapter in the general area titled Gateways and Thresholds. Was her mother researching the portal? It couldn't be a coincidence.

Turning to Daffodil, she said, "This must have been one of the last books she read before she disappeared. It may hold clues to her disappearance. I need to read it."

Daffodil's brow crinkled but softened at the sight of Ping's determination. "Yes, you must take it. May it guide you to the information you seek."

"Were you present when my mother entrusted me to Aunt Iris?"

Daffodil looked stricken. "I stood by her side when she spoke of it, though the moment itself was not mine to witness. You slumbered in your crib at dawn, and by dusk you'd journeyed to safety. She didn't say it was your aunt who took you, but Iris was absent and so were you. Your name became a hushed secret within Pixiandria."

Before they left the Queen's chamber, Daffodil opened a drawer in the bedside table, reached in, pulling out the tiniest, beaded bracelet Ping had ever seen. She handed it to Ping. "Here, Princess. I think your mother would want you to have it."

Ping shook her head, pushing the bracelet away. "I don't want to take any of her personal things. People will think I stole it."

Daffodil's eyes widened. "Oh no! It belonged to you. It was your baby bracelet. Look, it has your name Peony spelled out in beads." She hesitated, then whispered, "I've seen your mother gazing at it many times, thinking of you. Attach it to your bottle necklace, and when you find her, she'll have no doubt that you are her Peony."

With tears in both of their eyes, Daffodil helped Ping place the tiny bracelet around her pixie dust bottle. "Thank you, dear Daffodil!"

CHAPTER 25

Through the Portal

In the heart of the sunlit afternoon, Ping nestled in a cozy chair, lost in the pages of the mystical book she'd discovered in her mother's chamber. A particular passage caught her attention, and she reread it, eyes wide. She sprang up and circled the room, deep in thought.

When her excitement had cooled, she called for Violetta. "Please ask Thorn to come quickly. Tell him I've stumbled on something incredible." Violetta soared from the room.

Ping waited for Thorn's arrival, her gaze fixed on the mysterious piece of paper with her mother's handwriting: Unguarded, Unprotected, Undefended, I expose you.

The chapter she had just read, "Gateways and Thresholds," echoed in her thoughts, "When the vulnerable protections have thus been released,

Unguarded, Unprotected, Undefended, I expose you. When relinquished and unchanged, this alone shall make known a gateway to realms of shadow and treasure." She thought she now understood her mother's note.

Thorn arrived, and Ping eagerly shared the riddle. She waved the paper. "I'm not sure what vulnerable protections have been released in the dungeons, but I'm positive this means they've awakened the portal."

Thorn nodded in solemn agreement.

"I have to check it out." She hesitated before she asked, "Will you come with me?"

Thorn stared at her, eyes wide. "I absolutely will. I wouldn't let you do this alone."

Ping rushed to her closet and pulled her dagger from a shelf, buckling it around her waist.

"I haven't brought a weapon," Thorn said. "But I can produce my wand if needed."

"I've had so little practice with my wand. I feel safer with my dagger by my side."

In a flurry of excitement, they set off to the dungeons, determined to uncover the truth.

With Thorn conjuring small light orbs to brighten their way, they descended to the deepest level where their previous adventure had halted.

"The portal has to be here!" Ping cried with both hope and urgency.

They searched the wall, but the stones revealed no hidden passageways.

Thorn's brow furrowed as he considered the problem. "What if we say the words? Perhaps the portal will appear."

"It couldn't be that easy, could it?" Her brow furrowed in disbelief. "We must be missing something."

They shared a glance and Ping pulled out the slip of paper. "Should we read it together?"

Thorn shook his head. "Only you. The book said 'unchanged' and there's less chance of error if one voice speaks."

With a nod of agreement, Ping drew a deep breath, and said in a voice clear and strong, "Unguarded, unprotected, undefended, I expose you."

Ping and Thorn waited in silence, scanning the unyielding walls and listening for any sound. Time stretched on, and silence reigned until, at last, a slender crack slowly appeared in the wall at the corridor's end. It stretched and expanded, revealing a portal, round and foreboding, a gateway to a land of shadows and intrigue.

With a whoosh and a whirl, the magical portal flung open, revealing swirling colors. Bright, bold hues of orange, purple, yellow, blue, and green danced before their eyes, shining with brilliance. Thorn's face was a canvas of wonder mixed with a sprinkle of nerves. His excitement and fear mirrored Ping's. Thorn reached out his hand, his fingers reminding Ping of friendly tree branches. She clasped it and squeezed encouragement, whispering, "Don't let go for any reason!"

Thorn gave a brisk nod, the hawthorn berries among his curls bouncing. "I've got you. Hang on tight."

With hearts pounding, they inhaled courage, set their jaws with fierce resolve, and launched themselves into the unknown. They found a world of profound darkness, devoid of the swirling lights that filled the threshold.

Thorn snapped his fingers, and a timid glow flickered to life above them. It was a shy little beacon that barely nudged away the shadows. He tried again and again, each snap a hopeful beat, but the light grew only a smidge brighter each time.

Ping joined in, her snap coaxing the light to be less tentative, but not yet bold. It dimly illuminated a long corridor, a twin to the one they'd just left. A cold draft brushed against their cheeks, carrying with it the scent of decaying leaves. The worn stone floor they flew above was as uneven as the walls. They explored, their small light source flickering and casting fleeting glimpses, revealing fragments of the ominous shadows that engulfed the corridor.

A hushed silence hung heavy in the air, broken only by the occasional creak in the distance, heightening their sense of unease. They didn't dare speak, not even the tiniest whisper.

Tall, arched doorways lined the corridor, their once ornate frames now weathered and cracked, as if time had taken its toll on the grandeur that once existed. All the doors were shut, and they didn't dare peek inside, not knowing who or what might lurk there.

As they ventured deeper along the passage, Thorn pointed to faint symbols etched into the walls, hinting at a history waiting to be unraveled. Ping flew closer and examined them. They weren't dwarf runes.

Still holding hands, they floated forward, with

Thorn gently snapping to keep their small light alive. Ping wished for a glowworm like Glimmer to light their way without a sound.

Thorn risked a whisper, his voice barely louder than a breath. "Wish we had a map."

"With a big red X where my mom and Zinnia are," Ping whispered back.

A chuckle escaped Thorn, quickly silenced by his hand covering his mouth.

A horn sounded somewhere in the distance. Ping squeezed Thorn's hand and whisked him up to the ceiling, extinguishing the small light.

Concealed in the shadows, they moved forward when they heard nothing else. That's when a door creaked open ahead, and a figure zipped out, casting a blinding light that made them squint.

Fortunately, they went unnoticed. The figure turned and flew away, leaving the door ajar. They waited a few moments and then approached the door. A soft golden light seeped through the open crack and beckoned them with a comforting embrace. They peeked inside. The room looked empty, but uncertainty lingered.

Thorn glided through the doorway. When he tried to pull Ping's hand away, she held on, fiercely waggling her head and whispering, "We're a team, and teams stick together."

Flying to a table in the room's center, they surveyed the space with a twirl. Empty dishes rested on the table, remnants of a past meal. Ping gave Thorn a puzzled shrug. He gestured toward the door, but before they could leave, a soft skittering sound brought their attention to a small mouse sneaking into the room.

Before she could stop herself, Ping cried, "Chia!"

Quick as a flash, Thorn clapped his hand over her mouth.

Chia paused, his whiskers twitching. Looking up at them, his tiny round eyes sparkling, he chittered, "Missy Ping, here you are!" He scurried further into the room and darted under the table.

Ping and Thorn fluttered down like two leaves falling from a tree and joined their unexpected companion.

Ping asked, "What are you doing here?"

"I followed you," Chia confessed, his eyes gleaming with loyalty. "When you opened the portal, I knew, know, know there might be trouble ahead. I'm here to lend a paw!"

Warmth filled Ping's heart at the sight of her brave little friend. "Chia, it's too dangerous. You shouldn't be here."

"Where is 'here' exactly?" Chia asked, his nose wiggling with curiosity.

"We're not sure ourselves, but we're guessing it's the Dark Lands." Ping realized Thorn was staring at her, face puzzled. "Oh my, you can't understand Chia's chittering!" She repeated the mouse's words, ending with, "Chia's my friend."

Thorn shrugged. "Can he understand me?"

Ping looked at Chia, who nodded.

Thorn peered down at the mouse. "Always happy to meet Ping's friends, Chia. I'm Thorn."

Chia nodded proudly. "Yes, yes, yes, I'm a friend and I protect her. What do you do?"

Ping translated.

"Actually, nothing yet. I'm still figuring out my purpose in all this. But I'll get there, eventually."

Ping scanned the shadows, her gaze darting like a butterfly. "If Queen Aster is here, we don't know where she is."

Chia said, "Leave it to me. I've brought some spider spies, and we'll scout around."

He squeaked, and two spiders crept from a small crack in the wall. Chia dashed over to speak with them before they jumped and crawled back through the crack. He sprinted to the table. "We'll hide and wait. They'll explore and report."

Chia snuggled into a cozy corner.

Ping pointed to a chair seat. She and Thorn took refuge on it as they awaited news from their eight-legged scouts.

Ping's eyelids drooped with fatigue, the day's adventures catching up with her, but the fear of being discovered by someone dangerous kept her alert. The Dark Lands appeared to be a maze of hallways rather than a kingdom. Not what she expected. Doubts crept into her thoughts. She'd been right about the portal, but where were her mother and Lady Zinnia? Were they even in this strange place? Was it a senseless mission? She shook the doubts away. Their mission was far from senseless. It was a quest for the truth, and quests were never for the fainthearted.

Beside her, Thorn snoozed away, his snores gentle and

rhythmic, unfazed by the worries marching through Ping's mind. She poked him in the arm, and he snorted awake. She shook her head, her eyes wide with a silent plea for quiet.

Before long, they heard tiny feet scrabbling on the stone floor. The two diligent spiders made their way to Chia, their movements quick and purposeful. After a hushed conversation, Chia scrutinized the room and then shot across to the table with his spies close behind. He scaled the chair leg with ease and peered at the two Pixies.

"They couldn't find any sign of the Queen or the mean lady," he reported. "But they spotted the guards' location and found a door leading outside. Do you want to go there?"

Ping relayed the message to Thorn, who whispered, "Dare we?"

"I think we must. Queen Aster and Lady Zinnia could be in danger. We've come too far to turn back now."

"And if we find ourselves locked out?"

"We won't know until we've tried."

Thorn shrugged. "I'm ready for anything—I think. Let's go before we lose our nerve."

Ping turned to Chia. "Maybe you should stay here. If trouble finds us, you could seek help."

Chia tilted his head, considering. "I could, but who would I seek? You're the only faery who understands me."

"That's true."

Chia chittered, and the spiders crept closer.

"I'm Spinet," said one and hopped into the pocket Ping held open.

"And I'm Webwick," said the other.

Ping explained the conversation to Thorn while lifting Chia to perch on her shoulder. Thorn offered Webwick a pocket as well, scooping him up and placing him inside.

Everyone secure, they slipped cautiously into the hallway. Following the directions of their clever spider guides, they dodged the guard stations with ease.

Soon, they stood before a door leading to the unknown outdoors. A single lock at the top of the door hinted it was meant for those with wings. Thorn twisted the lock and cracked open the door enough to peek through. Fog shrouded the world outside, the air biting cold. They hadn't brought coats or hats. Could they survive the chill? If they wanted to explore, they'd have to try.

Chia suggested they wait a bit. He whispered to the spiders, who scrambled out of the pockets, climbed down the door, and vanished into the corridor. They returned with news of clothing hung on hooks in the hall that might fit Ping and Thorn.

The pixies followed the spiders and discovered pixie hats and coats hanging on wall hooks, with boots on the floor beneath.

They bundled in their newfound garments with Spinet, Webwick, and Chia tucked comfortably in pockets. Returning to the door, they peeked out again.

"What if we're walking into a trap?" Ping wondered aloud.

"Could be," Thorn said. "We need to be prepared for anything."

The darkness loomed, the cold beckoned, and the unknown called to them. Yet, with hearts full of courage and determination to find Queen Aster and Lady Zinnia, they tiptoed outside, leaving the warmth of the corridors.

CHAPTER 26

Earthshake

Frigg, Tip, Iris, and Cricall had been traveling for three days, hoping they'd eventually reach Pixiandria. Each day, Iris would dash ahead and return to reassure them of the route. But Frigg had doubts. Iris had admitted her trusty doves always navigated. Without them, their path was guided by Iris's whimsical notion that Pixiandria lay "over there somewhere." Frigg longed for a map!

As they crossed a meadow as wide as the sky itself, Cricall seized the moment to gallop and frolic among the swaying grasses. Tip gathered daisies and released their petals into the air, watching them twirl down like a flurry of snowflakes. Meanwhile, Frigg scoured the ground for wild carrots for their evening meal.

Then the earth started rumbling. First, the land moaned from its depths, as though it had a bellyache. Then the surrounding field waltzed and tumbled—left and right, up and down, side to side. A nasty odor, like a foul-smelling troll, rose from its depths.

"Earthshake!" Tip shouted.

Frigg froze, her memories whisking her back to a time when she was just a dwarfling. She'd been in her cozy bedroom inside the mountain when the world had quivered and rocked, jiggling and jogging all around her. Her toys had taken flight from their shelves, and she had burrowed under her bed, clutching at the floor.

When the shaking stopped, she was too afraid to peek out until her father found her. He hugged her tightly and whispered that everything would be fine. "It was the mountain laughing at a joke the sun told."

Frigg remembered thinking the sun should keep its humor to itself.

This time, the shaking terrified her. There was no place to hide. She dropped to the rolling ground, her fingers weaving through the grass, searching for an anchor.

Iris hovered, untouched by the earthbound tremors, her expression one of bewildered concern.

Tip dropped to the ground near Frigg and offered her a brave smile, though a shadow of fear flickered behind it.

Frigg searched for Cricall. He stood firm, his legs braced wide, trying to outlast the earthshake. But the earth had other plans, and the ground beneath him lurched. With a startled yelp, he sunk into the ground.

The shaking slowed and then stopped. Frigg and Tip forgot their fear and sprang into action, rushing to Cricall's aid as he called out for help.

"Shaking shales, Cric, what happened?" Concern filled Frigg's voice.

Iris circled Cricall's head, her wings a blur. "He's toppled into a hole! Silly unicorn." Her head shook, though her eyes were laced with worry.

Cricall tried to free himself, but the soil held him captive, his legs buried halfway. Dirt and rocks formed a trap from which he couldn't pull himself free. "I'm stuck," he said, distress in his voice. "One of my back legs is hurting, but I can't turn to heal it."

"Stay still, Cric," Tip advised. "You don't want to injure yourself more. We'll free you."

"The rope?" Frigg asked, her mind racing for solutions.

"That could be handy," Tip agreed, "but we need something to make a ramp. Something strong and flat."

Cricall had calmed himself. "I'll be still as a statue. Wouldn't want to snap a leg."

The trio scattered, searching for a solution. They didn't notice the small creature until it piped up, "Um, excuse me, please."

Frigg turned to find an animal with white fur and black spots. The creature's long black ears tilted forward, and it nibbled a carrot as it assessed the situation.

"Hello," Frigg said. "We're kind of busy. Can we chat later?"

The creature tapped its foot. "Um, well, you see, it's rather urgent we speak NOW!"

Everyone stopped, turning their attention to the newcomer.

Frigg apologized. "I'm sorry we weren't listening to you, but our friend is stuck in a hole. After we free him, we can sit and talk."

The creature said, "Your friend isn't just stuck in a hole. He's stuck in my home."

The friends exchanged surprised glances.

"Oh dear," Tip murmured, peering at Cricall and then down at the trench that used to be the rabbit's tunnels. "We're truly sorry about that."

Iris flew over to the creature. "We'll have him out of your home in no time."

The creature sighed, its whiskers twitching with a hint of distress. "I appreciate that, but freeing your friend is only the beginning. Fixing my roof is the next challenge, and how I'll manage it, I have no idea."

Frigg said, "Well, okay, let's tackle this problem one step at a time. We'll get Cric out of your home and back on solid ground. Then we'll fix your roof."

The creature's face scrunched up. "Fine. But you realize my home is a bunch of tunnels under the entire field, right? Didn't he know he was too heavy to walk over a field filled with rabbit burrows?"

Frigg smiled, recognizing the word. "Ah, so you're a rabbit. I've heard tales about rabbits."

Iris huffed, her wings fluttering. "And didn't you know not to dig your tunnels next to the surface so someone heavy wouldn't fall into them?"

The rabbit's ears drooped. It sat, looking quite sad. "Nobody's around to teach me. All my relatives are gone."

Frigg patted its shoulder. "I'm so sorry about your loss."

"Loss, what loss? I was glad to be rid of them. They kicked me out because my snowy fur made it too easy for predators to see me. They were afraid I'd bring the humans down on them. But I'd never dug tunnels before."

Tip said, "Well, the earthshake didn't help."

"Excuse me," Cricall said, "remember me? I'm the unicorn who needs rescuing. Your story is very sad, but I'm still stuck in this trench, um, I mean, your home, and I'd really like to get out."

Tip hurried to Cricall's side. "We haven't forgotten you. Let's find something to create a ramp for your escape."

The rabbit perked up. "I know just the thing. Follow me." It jumped, did a twist in midair, and hopped away, with Iris flying close behind.

Iris returned shortly, excitement shining on her face. "I think the rabbit's got it!"

"Got what?" Tip asked, craning his neck to see.

"C'mon, I'll show you." Iris motioned for Tip and Frigg to follow.

They ran after her, across the field as they picked their way around caved-in rabbit tunnels. Ahead, they saw a partially built structure. The rabbit hopped around a gigantic pile of long boards scattered haphazardly near the structure.

"What is this place?" Frigg stared nervously at the unfinished building.

"It's a human house. They use these boards to build them. Living above ground—can you imagine?"

Frigg froze. "Humans? They're nearby?"

"Yep, humans are everywhere."

Tip glanced around. "You've seen them?"

"Sure have. Every day."

Shivers traveled up Frigg's back. She glanced at the worried faces of Tip and Iris. "Let's get Cric free as fast as we can!"

"Fine with me," Iris agreed.

The rabbit pulled a board loose with her teeth.

"Wow, you're strong!" Tip cried.

With a modest grunt, the rabbit replied. "You need tough teeth and sturdy paws to burrow through the stubborn soil. Uh, I could use some help here."

Frigg grabbed the loose end of the flat, rough wood. Tip grabbed the other end, and with the rabbit supporting the middle, they hurried back across the field. When they reached Cricall, Frigg set her end of the board down and wiped the sweat from her forehead with her sleeve.

"We're going to need another board to make the ramp wide enough," Tip said.

So, they rushed back and brought a second board. After they'd rested, Tip maneuvered the boards in place, forming a ramp in front of Cricall. Frigg jumped into the hole and scooped the dirt and rocks away from their friend's legs.

"Lift your front hooves to make sure they're okay," Tip said. "Then you can walk slowly onto the ramp."

"Stop!" a voice called. The rabbit hopped forward and examined the ramp. "We need dirt packed under those boards for support or they might break from his weight." She jumped in and started digging dirt from the side with her front legs and kicking it under the ramp with her back legs. Frigg and Tip pressed the soil into a hard base under the ramp.

When it was as sturdy as they could make it, Cricall rested his front hooves on the boards and wobbled up to ground level, limping off with a relieved whinny.

"Phew! Thought I was stuck for good."

"We'd never leave you behind," Frigg assured, throwing her arms around his neck.

Tip frowned. "You're hobbling. Are you sure you're okay?"

"My legs are bruised and that back one is hurting, but I think I can heal them enough to travel."

Iris landed on his head and playfully tousled his mane. "Silly unicorn," she teased.

Cricall turned to the rabbit. "Thank you ever so much for your help, uh, rabbit."

"My name is Speckles. Because of the black spots on my white fur, you see."

"Pleased to meet you, Speckles." Frigg reached out her hand to shake the rabbit's paw. She noticed the delicate features and fur ruff under her chin distinguishing Speckles as a doe. She introduced everyone.

"Well, now that you've got your unicorn free, let's check the damage to my tunnels."

They peered into the hole and surveyed the surrounding field, noting the dips and deep trenches where the earthshake had caved in Speckles' home.

"This is an enormous repair job," Tip said. "Usually there are more shakes after an earthshake. Although they'll be weaker, your new tunnels will probably collapse again."

Speckles slumped onto the ground, her long lashes casting shadows over her eyes. "You're right," she said. "My tunneling skill needs work. Guess I'd better start over."

"But will you be safe?" Frigg asked. "The humans are so close."

Speckles' ears quivered. "Probably not, but where else can I go?"

Frigg turned to Tip. "Any ideas?"

"Underground is safer, but she'll have to come out to forage for food." Tip thought for a moment and then shook his head. "I'm afraid her relatives were right. Her white fur won't blend into the surroundings. The humans, wolves, or hawks are bound to see her."

Iris fluttered down, settling on Speckles' shoulder. She used her skirt to gently dab the tear trailing down the rabbit's face. "Why don't you come with us, dear?"

"What a wonderful idea!" Frigg said.

Speckles' ears perked straight up, curiosity gleaming in her eyes. "Where are you heading?"

Frigg explained their mission. "Perhaps we'll stumble on a cozy place for you to live."

Iris said, "Of course, if you could tunnel your way into Pixiandria, we'd avoid the front gate."

Tip laughed. "Yes, but we're a tad bit large for rabbit-sized tunnels."

"And they'd probably cave in on you," Speckles chuckled. She paused, her whiskers twitching with an idea. "Why not take the back way?"

Iris's eyes widened. "I've lived in Pixiandria all my life and never heard of a back way."

Speckles said, "My Uncle Ferbie mentioned it when he fetched magical medicine from the faeries for my cousin. He slipped in the back way to meet with the healer."

Frigg leaned in. "What else did he say?"

"Just that it's a shadowy path, quite eerie."

"Whoa!" Cricall cried, "Not fond of eerie."

"A powerful enchantment guards the bridge entrance. I remember because he said it shrinks you so you're not bigger than the faeries." Speckles giggled. "I couldn't imagine a tiny Uncle Ferbie."

Tip said, "That sounds ideal. Do you think you could find it?"

"I'm willing to try," Speckles said with newfound determination.

Frigg hugged her. "Please come."

Cricall added, "After we rescue our dear friend Ping, we'll help you find a safe place to live. After all, I destroyed your home."

"The earthshake played its part, too," Iris reminded him.

A smile replaced Speckles' despair. "Yes, I'll come with you. It'll be lovely to have friends to share the journey."

Frigg clapped her hands. "Okay, then we're off to find Ping and secure Speckles a home."

With that, the friends continued their journey, their steps buoyed by the addition of a new ally and a noble purpose to spur them on.

CHAPTER 27

The Back Way

Cricall munched a mouthful of grass, the vibrant green blades sticking out of his lips as he rested with the others in a lush meadow. "This grass is splendid."

"Yes, it's scrumptious," Speckles agreed, her nose buried in the greenery. "These dandypuffs are especially tasty."

"Dandypuffs?" Frigg asked, eyeing the cheerful yellow blossoms in front of Speckles. "They're good to eat?"

"Absolutely!" Speckles nudged a bloom toward Frigg. "Especially the flowers. They're like a burst of sunshine. Here, try one."

Iris glided over, alighting between Speckles' ears. She reached out, plucking the flower from the rabbit's paw, and buried her nose into the center. "Smells like joy!" Sampling a petal, she twirled with glee. She stuffed more petals into her mouth and grinned, yellow dandypuff juice dribbling down her chin.

Frigg sampled a dandypuff flower. "A pinch of rock salt would enhance it, but otherwise it's a delicious treat."

Cricall said, "The leaves are even better."

Tip found them, "Delectable, with a savory tang."

Soon everyone busily harvested dandypuffs, filling a sack with the golden bounty for their journey ahead.

Speckles wrinkled her nose. "The yellow flowers lose their charm when they turn into white puffs that float on the wind. It's like eating a mouthful of feathers."

"It's our good fortune to have discovered them before that happened," Tip said with a grin.

Frigg said, "Speckles, we know about carrots and dandypuffs. Could you show us other things we can eat?"

"I most certainly can." Speckles' ears straightened with enthusiasm. "The meadow is a banquet if you open your eyes."

"Well," Iris said, "you can open them for us."

The breeze shifted, and an unfamiliar odor assailed them. "Pe-ew! What is that dreadful smell?" Tip asked, his nose twitching. "It smells like something died."

With a sprightly leap, Cricall rushed to investigate. But the overpowering stench forced him to stumble backward, his keen unicorn nostrils flaring in disgust. "It's like the odor of old hay left in a damp field to rot."

Speckles hopped over and warned, "Don't touch it! That's a stinky bush. Not a treat for nose or mouth."

Frigg couldn't help but laugh. "It certainly lives up

to its name. A real nose-wrinkler! It reeks like decaying mushrooms!"

The gang edged cautiously away from the bush, its variegated leaves waving in the breeze and releasing even more pungency.

Iris soared above the smell and drifted off. "I'm going in search of more joyful scents."

Tip wrinkled his nose. "I won't ever forget that awful odor means stay away!"

Speckles gave a wise nod. "Absolutely! But a feast of more delightful smells awaits us over there." She hopped through the field, sharing the joys of buttery clover, honeyed purple flowers, and sugary orange poppies. "We'll find berry bushes and fruit trees along the way."

After quenching their thirst at a crystal-clear stream and refilling their canteens, they resumed their adventure, their spirits as lighthearted as the clouds above.

Later, as they went on their way, Speckles paused in the intersection of four roads, studying the paths crossing before her.

Tip asked, "Are we lost?"

She tilted her head and pointed her paw to the right. "No. Let's go this way."

"Are you sure?" Frigg asked, her gaze flitting toward Iris for a second opinion.

"Not exactly," Speckles said. Her voice trailing off for a moment as she pondered the question. "Remember, I've never been to Pixiandria."

Cricall suggested, "Let's take a break to get our bearings."

"Not a bad idea. I'll have a quick look ahead." Iris soared into the direction Speckles had chosen. Soon she was only a dot in the distance.

Speckles watched in amazement. "My, she's not one to dilly-dally, is she?"

Tip laughed. "Nope, she's like a flash of lightning."

They strolled into the welcoming shade of nearby trees while they waited.

Frigg reached into her pack and retrieved her cloth runes bag. Eyes closed, she whispered, "Odin and Freya, please show us the way." Then she reached into the bag and pulled out a rune. "Eihwaz," she announced.

Eihwaz

Speckles peer closer. "What's that?"

"It's a rune," Frigg explained. "A symbol of defense and protection."

Tip's head swiveled to stare at Frigg with wide eyes. "Does it mean a fight is ahead?"

Frigg considered. "It's possible. But Eihwaz also represents the yew tree, a symbol of life."

Speckles nodded thoughtfully. "Life is good. Much better than death."

Cricall laughed. "That's for sure!"

"But what does a rune do?" Speckles asked.

"Runes are ancient symbols that carry messages from the gods, especially Odin, the god of all, and Freya, the goddess of love," Frigg said. "They guide us and provide inspiration."

"So, they tell you what's going to happen?" Speckles' eyes filled with intrigue.

"No. They offer advice, not predictions. Interpreting their meaning is a bit like solving a puzzle."

Speckles wrinkled her brow, thinking, and then nodded in understanding.

A fresh idea struck Frigg, and she reached into the bag again. "Odin and Freya, please show us how our friend Ping is doing."

Tip bounced with excitement. "What does it mean? Is she okay?"

"Give me a moment to think!" Frigg said as she examined the rune she'd selected from the bag. "It's Berkanan. It means growth."

Berkanan

The rune left Frigg with a mixture of hope and uncertainty. She was frantic for more information about Ping. What was happening to her? Was she scared? This was the longest she'd ever been apart from Ping. Worried didn't begin to describe the emotion Frigg felt.

Iris brought Frigg out of her thoughts and back to reality when the faery returned and confirmed they were on the correct path. She'd recognized some landmarks.

Their spirits lifted, and they rose to their feet, energized and ready to continue their quest.

Later in the day, they approached a weathered stone bridge adorned with moss that arched over a stream as green and sluggish as a sleepy turtle.

Speckles bounced up and down. "This is it! It's just like Uncle Ferbie described—yucky water and huge colored stones. He said they make you feel tingly as you pass."

Tip eyed the bridge with suspicion. "It looks unstable."

Frigg said, "I'm nervous about those giant gemstones that make you tingly!"

Iris zipped across the bridge and returned, her laughter trailing behind her. "Pixie crystals filled with magic."

Speckles' eyes grew round. "Magic? Are they what made Uncle Ferbie shrink to the size of a pixie?"

"Hard to tell. Their magic is boundless," Iris replied.

With a worried look, Cricall moved closer to the bridge. "Stay here until I've checked it out." After a close inspection, Cricall reported, "There are huge gaps where stones have tumbled into the murky depths below."

Tip and Frigg shared a pained glance and whispered in unison, "Banaga Canyon..."

Iris landed on Frigg's shoulder. "What's a banagan?"

"Banaga," Tip replied. "It's a treacherous canyon inside our mountain. The rocky bridge over its deep canyon was about as risky as this one."

Frigg nodded. "We had no choice but to cross it."

Cricall swallowed hard. "I remember. Frigg nearly fell."

Iris fluttered and faced them. "Well, a fall here would only mean a splash in the stream, not a plunge of doom."

Speckles frowned. "Unless the water is enchanted and turns us into toads."

Tip grimaced. "Or leathery lizards."

Frigg scowled. "Or perhaps slithering snakes."

"You'd be leathery, slithery, or toads, but you'd still be alive," Iris said with a giggle.

Cricall crinkled his nose. "The water smells nasty, like that stinky bush! My horn can clean dirty water, but I don't think it could fix that mess!"

Darkness was all Frigg saw across the bridge. She couldn't make out shapes. A foreboding seized her, but she squared her shoulders. "Nasty or not, it's a gamble we need to take to find Ping."

Tip said, "We chose risky when we came."

Frigg took a deep breath. "I'll go first. If I fall or turn into a toad, you'll have to rescue me." She stepped onto the bridge, weaving around the gaping holes. As she neared the first pixie crystal, it pulsated with a soft blue light and the air crackled. A peculiar sensation washed over her, rippling from her head to her toes. Holes in the bridge now resembled canyons surrounded by boulders, and it took her a lot more steps to go around them. She glanced back at her friends. They stared at her, puzzlement carved on their faces.

"You're shrinking!" Tip called out in alarm.

From above her, Iris confirmed, "Yes, you're becoming petite as a pixie with each step!"

Frigg said, "That's their magic! They're shrinking crystals."

After safely crossing the bridge, she turned and shouted, "I made it!"

Her friends followed the same winding path Frigg had used to cross the bridge. She watched them gradually shrink.

They gazed at each other, filled with wonder at their newfound stature.

Speckles giggled. "I'm littler compared to you!"

"And I'm small, but still a bit bigger than all of you," Cricall said.

Tip stared at Iris, hovering next to him. "I'm Iris-sized!"

"I hope we can find a way to turn us back," Frigg grumbled.

CHAPTER 28

A Light in the Dark

When the friends peered into the shadowy forest, their mood sobered. An intimidating haze infused with the scent of decaying leaves loomed over the path ahead.

"It's like the bridge acted as a gateway between light and darkness," Frigg said in a hushed tone.

They glanced back at the world behind them, bathed in warm, inviting sunlight. As they turned toward the path ahead, cloaked in mysterious twilight, they shivered.

Tip broke the silence with a question. "Isn't it odd nobody guards the path? Would they let wanderers enter without a challenge?"

Iris bit her lip. "It's most unusual. Pixiandria is well guarded. This place must lie beyond Pixiandria's borders."

"It could have defenses we can't see," Cricall said.

Frigg nodded. "Like magic safeguards or spells."

Tip asked, "Iris, have you ever flown over these lands?"

"No, I've never traveled here."

Frigg and Tip exchanged confused glances. "Never?" Frigg asked. "Earlier, you said you recognized some landmarks on the way here."

"Oh, did I? Guess I was mistaken," Iris said with a casual wave of her hand.

"Mistaken?" Tip cried. "We trusted your word!"

"I don't travel much. Have to be careful because I'm tiny, you know. Might be mistaken for a bug to swat."

Frigg thought about the strange places they'd traveled to find Anasgar, thrilling but dangerous. Being this small in a world so vast, she'd be cautious as well. No wonder Ping had sought refuge in Frigg's pocket so often.

Tip voiced his uncertainty. "If this isn't Pixiandria, why did the pixie crystals make us small?"

Cricall added, "And how will we find Pixiandria from here? We don't know where we are."

Speckles ears stood upright. "My uncle found his way after crossing the tingly bridge. This must be the path to what he called the Dark Lands. I didn't know I'd come here, or I'd have asked more questions."

"I suggest we keep going and watch for clues," Frigg said.

Iris studied the gloomy route ahead. "The bridge's magic wouldn't have altered your size without purpose. It left me unchanged, so it recognized my pixieness. Let's go and see what happens."

"I hope whatever happens is good," Tip grumbled.

Cricall stamped his foot. "Remember, we're here to rescue Ping!"

"Yes," Frigg shouted. "Rescue Ping!"

They all repeated, "Rescue Ping!"

As they ventured deeper along the mysterious path, Frigg noted the trees seemed much bigger. They weren't reduced. This world seemed to be a darkened version of the world they had come from.

A sudden gust of wind swept through the trees, causing the branches to sway and creak, as if nature itself warned them of the dangers ahead. Frigg shivered, unable to shake off the sensation of unseen eyes watching them.

It wasn't long before a faint light pierced the darkness and slowly grew. Frigg searched for the light's source. "Let's get off the path. It may not be safe for us here."

"The darkness is thick with the trees so tightly packed," Iris said. "That's spookier than some light."

Tip agreed. "Yeah."

Frigg's whisper was insistent, her heart racing. She realized their window of opportunity to seek safety was closing with each passing moment. "We must hide until we know what it is."

"I'll find out." Iris soared toward the mysterious light.

They waited.

Suddenly, Iris's voice fluttered down from above them, urgent and strong. "Hide!"

Frigg sprang into action. "Run this way!"

They staggered into the forest, the haze so thick they could feel its icy chill but not see each other.

Frigg shivered from the cold. Or was it from fear? Maybe both. Doubts crept in like unwelcome phantoms. Had her choice been a mistake? Where could they hide?

"I can't see where I'm going!" Cricall said in a low voice.

Tip whispered, "This fogginess stinks!"

An idea sparked within Frigg as she recalled the stinky bush they'd found earlier. She chanted in a low voice, "I'm a stinky bush. I'm a stinky bush. I'm a stinky bush." Her body twisted and stretched. Her bones and muscles grumbled until she became the very plant she envisioned. Before the pain subsided, she urged her friends, "Inside, quickly!"

Everyone found her by the pungent aroma. Pushing through her leafy disguise, they huddled within the bush's branches. She had to stretch a bit more to get Cricall's whole body inside, but soon, everyone was covered.

Frigg felt for the dagger at her waist. If all else failed, she could fight.

Tip grimaced. "Ugh, that odor is fierce!"

Iris hushed him. "Hold your breath."

The light prowled around them, its brilliance piercing the fog, but revealing nothing about its bearer.

Abruptly, the branches of Frigg's stinky bush swooshed as a massive snout thrust them aside. Frigg's heart raced. She stifled a scream and a longing to peek, fearing what she might see.

Time stretched on, each second an eternity as the creature snuffled around the area. At last, the giant nose lost interest, and the beacon of light drifted away.

They remained motionless, silent statues in a foul-smelling bush, until Speckles signaled the all-clear, "I think it's gone."

The friends scrambled from the Frigg bush, shaking off the scent and the fear.

Frigg repeated the chant to transform her body. "I'm a dwarf, I'm a dwarf, I'm a dwarf." She grimaced with effort as she changed.

Speckles' eyes sparkled with wonder. "That was amazing!"

Frigg gave a sheepish grin. "Surprise! I had to act fast, and that bush was the first thing I thought of."

"You're our smelly hero," Speckles giggled.

"Brilliant move, Frigg! You're as clever as you are quick," Cricall said.

"Aromatic, but it worked," Iris chuckled merrily.

Tip peered through the lifting fog. "Uh, that odor is lingering. Can we move on?"

"I hope it's only the smell of the air, not me!" Frigg grumbled as they returned to the path.

Speckles searched out Iris, who circled above. "What was that creature?"

Iris floated in front of them. "It was enormous, with ivory tusks, and a lantern-shaped light attached to its snout."

Tip chuckled. "A lantern-nosed beast?"

Iris placed her hands on her hips and a frown on her lips. "It was huge and scary, no laughing matter."

Cricall said thoughtfully, "If you live in a dark forest, such a light would be helpful. You'd never lose your way."

Frigg teased, "Maybe a lantern for your horn would be useful, Cric."

"Do you think the creature was friendly?" Speckles asked.

Iris shook her head. "Judging by its gigantic teeth, probably not."

"I'd say it's best to keep our distance," Frigg said. "Let's move on before it returns."

No one argued, but the mystery of the lantern-nosed creature lingered in their minds.

CHAPTER 29

Tower without a Door

Ping and Thorn emerged from the building into the unknown landscape outside. Webwick, Spinet, and Chia nestled cozily in their pockets. An icy fog blanket hugged the world around them and swallowed the path ahead. Their wings, lying snug against their backs under the coats they'd found inside, yearned to flutter free.

"Hard to fly when you can't see where you're going," Ping said through chattering teeth. "And this chilly air makes it hard to talk."

Thorn nodded but agreed by keeping his mouth closed and the cold out.

"You okay in there?" Ping asked Chia and Spinet, nestled deep inside her pocket.

"Snug as a hug," piped a tiny voice.

"How about you, Webwick?"

Ping made out the whisper from Thorn's pocket,

"Still alive!"

Their feet carried them forward over the dirt path. They saw nothing, but often heard furtive rustling sounds around them.

Thorn finally spoke, his voice hopeful. "The fog is drifting away."

Ping smiled as she realized Thorn was correct. "And the air has lost some of its bite."

The fog's retreat quickened their pace despite the weight of unfamiliar coats, hats, and boots. But the departing mist also revealed shapes moving in the underbrush near the path. A sudden rustle, a dash across their trail. A small creature, perhaps?

"Hey, Chia, you may have relatives here," Ping teased.

"I'll come out, out, out and meet them later, after things warm up."

As they moved deeper into the strange landscape, the cold's grip loosened, a subtle warmth seeping under their coats' layers. Chia dared a peek from his cozy pocket. "What's over there?"

Beyond a bushy thicket, a stone structure loomed, silent and imposing. "It looks like a tower," Thorn said.

They stumbled through the shrubs and small trees to stand before the peculiar tower, its eight-sides stretching skyward. No doors or windows offered entrance. Everything about the tower screamed, "PRISON!"

If it wasn't a prison and they didn't find Queen Aster and Lady Zinnia inside, they might find a clue to their whereabouts. Ping and Thorn exchanged glances, their eyes wide with curiosity.

They circled the tower. Finding nothing, Ping asked Thorn, "Do you know any magic to reveal a door?"

"I'm not sure. I can locate lost objects, but I'm willing to give a missing door a try." He held out his hand, and a wand materialized. A colorful leaf graced the end. He concentrated on the tower and waved his wand. Nothing opened and no door magically appeared.

He looked so disappointed, Ping tried to cheer him with a smile. "So, boy faeries have leaf wands? I got a star on mine, not a girl's flower."

"The royal family has star wands."

"Oh," was all Ping could manage.

"That's amazingly special!" a tiny voice said.

"Chia," Ping said, addressing the tiny creature peeking from her pocket, "any brilliant ideas for finding a door?"

"If there's a crack for me to squeeze through, I might find a door inside to let you in."

"Worth a try," Thorn said, stretching out his hand.

Chia hopped into it and was lowered to the ground. The little mouse scurried toward the tower, disappearing around its base. When he returned, his eyes sparkled with excitement. "I found it! There's a gap. Follow me."

They rushed around the building, stopping abruptly when Chia halted before a miniscule hole.

Ping frowned. "That's dinky. Can you squeeze through there? Looks like a spider job to me."

Spinet and Webwick crept from pockets, skittering down Ping and Thorn to the ground.

Chia said, "I may need spider help to clear out some rocks if the wall is super thick."

Thorn patted Chia's head with his finger and nodded to the spiders. "You've got this, tiny friends."

Chia wiggled through the hole with Spinet and Webwick following. Soon, a little rock emerged. Thorn reached down and pulled it out, bringing Chia with it.

"Hey! Warn a mouse before you yank his rock away!"

Thorn blushed. "Sorry, I was trying to help."

"More rocks block the way. I'll fetch them, and you can pull, pull, pull to your heart's content."

With surprise, Ping realized Thorn was talking to Chia. She asked, "When did you start understanding the critters?"

Thorn's surprised look told her he hadn't noticed it until now, either. "I don't know. It just happened."

"Huh, interesting." Ping thought about The Ancient One's belief that pixies develop the skills they need.

After Chia had maneuvered two more rocks through the hole, they heard nothing from him for quite a few minutes.

Ping worried. "Should we call to him?"

"Not yet. We don't want to attract attention to him if someone's on the other side."

Ping chewed her lip and her hair shimmered a nervous purple.

Finally, with a tiny whisker wiggle, Chia poked his head back through the opening. "I found a door. It's next to this hole. Magic must be hiding it from the outside. I haven't figured out how to open it, so I'll join the spiders exploring the tower."

Ping hesitated. "It might be dangerous."

Chia chuckled. "I thrive on danger! Be back in a jiffy."

With a flip of his tail, he vanished once more into the tower. Time stretched on. Suddenly, the air filled with the hum of buzzing wings. Someone was coming.

Ping and Thorn exchanged a quick glance. Thorn grabbed Ping's hand and pulled her behind a near-by bush, their bodies folding into the greenery. They peered through the leaves.

The buzzing grew louder, and Ping's mind raced with possibilities. How many faeries could there be? Two sturdy boots came into view, hovering before their leafy spyhole. Boots? The guards wore boots. The man's face remained unseen, but his presence was commanding as he chanted, "Open for the Lord of Pix-iandria."

Ping held back a gasp and wondered if Thorn had recognized it, too. He'd have to. What boy wouldn't know his own father's voice?

The screeching of a door scraping the stones inter-rupted her thoughts. However, before they could think what to do next, hands yanked them from their hiding place.

Lord Sycamore wasn't alone. He had an accom-plice! And that companion's grip was unyielding as they struggled. "What have we here? Spies?" Lord Sycamore sneered at Ping and his son. "Come. You can join Aster and Zinnia inside. Isn't that why you're here?"

Mouth opened wide in shock, Thorn cried, "Father, no! How could you do this?"

Sycamore's voice dripped with mockery. "Why, it's all for you, my son. When I'm Pixiandria's King Sycamore, you will be a prince. Together, we will rule the realm."

Sycamore grabbed Thorn. "This one's mine, Evergreen. You keep the Princess. She's vital to our plan. She may have caused a stir, but we can turn it in our favor."

His gaze locked on Ping, his words tinged with threat. "Princess, I'd hoped you'd be more like your Aunt Iris—silly and easy to control. But you are too smart for your own good."

Ping struggled and shouted, "No! Let me go!"

Lord Evergreen clutched her tighter, and Sycamore said, "Quit fighting. Should any misfortune befall you, I'll simply say you rejected Pixiandria and fled to that hideous dwarf colony where you belong."

They entered the tower. The door closed with a thunderous bang, sealing their fate within the mysterious walls.

CHAPTER 30

Outside the Tower

Frigg and her friends rounded a curve in the path. They glimpsed two pixies flying ahead. The thrill of discovering faeries made them eager to shout a greeting. But Iris's firm head shake silenced them. She gestured toward the sheltering trees beside the path.

"Quickly, before they spot us," she whispered, leading them deeper into the woods to a small clearing. They huddled close, their heads almost touching as they spoke in hushed tones.

Frigg asked, "Why did you move us off the path?"

Iris hadn't looked this serious since the day Ping was kidnapped. "Those were no ordinary pixies. That was Lord Sycamore and Lord Evergreen. Sycamore was the pixie who snatched Ping."

Tip frowned. "Why are they here?"

"Maybe they're up to mischief." Cricall's expression darkened.

Frigg's anger flared. "We should follow them. If they're involved in kidnapping Ping, they'll know where she is."

Iris said. "I'll scout ahead."

"No, they might see you," Tip objected.

Speckles hopped to the center of their circle. "It should be me. I'm only a simple rabbit to them, a forest creature. They won't even notice me. You wait here. If I don't return, don't follow."

Cricall said, "We can't promise that. No matter what, we stick together."

"Yes," Frigg agreed. "We're friends, and we'll do our best to rescue you."

Speckles sighed, exasperation and affection in her eyes. "Well, you do what you must, even if it is hare-brained. But for now, stay put."

The wait seemed to take forever, like moss growing on a rock. The group eagerly leaned forward when Speckles returned, panting and wide-eyed.

"I found them. And I think I found your princess, too."

"Ping?" they asked in unison.

Speckles' expression dimmed. "Not great news, I'm afraid." She explained how she'd located the lords by a mysterious tower. "I observed them capturing two pixies—a boy and a girl they called the princess. They dragged them into the tower."

"Oh, no!" Iris cried.

Speckles' body trembled. "One boasted the princess was needed for their plan. It didn't sound hopeful."

Cricall rested his horn lightly on Speckles' head, sending calming vibrations to her.

"Ping's situation has gotten worse." Frigg's heart sank. "I thought it was Zinnia we had to worry about, but now there are a couple of lords also?"

Iris frowned. "They must be working together. Zinnia is cunning. She can convince anyone of anything. We need to be prepared."

"At least we know where Ping is," Tip said. "Now we just have to rescue her."

Frigg turned to Speckles. "Can you hide near the tower and observe? When the lords leave, come back for us."

Iris wrung her hands, worry etched on her face. "I can't believe this! Lord Sycamore has always been a noble pixie. Well, except for when he kidnapped Ping in Nadavir."

Speckles said, "Rabbits can pretend to be good and then turn on you when you least expect it. I learned that the hard way. I thought they were my friends. Some were family. I'll bet faeries can be the same way. We need to be super careful."

"Yeah, he's captured Ping twice," Cricall agreed. "I think he's shown who he is."

Everyone nodded. They'd faced danger and encountered bad guys before. They'd be cautious when they saved their friend.

Frigg walked in circles, her mind racing as fast as her feet. Her thoughts ticked toward one goal: rescuing her dear friend Ping from the menace in the ominous tower.

Ever since they'd stepped over the bridge into this shadowy realm, it had been a game of waiting and hiding.

But Frigg was not one to sit idly by—she was ready to spring into action, to do anything to ensure Ping's safety.

Speckles hopped back to them with news. "Those lords flew away. I didn't see anyone else, but who knows how many others might lurk inside the tower."

Frigg said, "Let's move closer."

Silent as tree shadows, they followed Speckles to a clump of bushes close to the mysterious tower where they hid out of sight.

"I nibbled flowers and grass all around the tower," Speckles admitted with a little burp, "but the door they used remains a mystery."

Iris twisted her hands together. "It must be cloaked by magic."

Tip nodded. "We need a clever plan, and we need it now. Those lords might swoop back any second with reinforcements."

Hatching a plan wasn't easy. The land was unfamiliar, the tower a riddle, and Ping's plight a tangled web they couldn't unravel.

"We must act," Iris said, her wings fluttering with exasperation. "I'll circle the tower. Perhaps I can find a tiny way in."

Frigg said, "Speckles didn't find any openings. What if guards catch you?"

Iris puffed with pride. "I wield a wand of magic, remember? If I understand the spells at work, I can weave a counter charm!" With a swoosh, she darted toward the tower, a brave spark against the dark sky.

CHAPTER 31

Inside the Tower

In the tower's highest room, an open loft with a meager light streaming through the single roof skylight offered little hope to Ping. Her head hurt, but she tried to stay awake. She needed to think. She'd set out to find her mother and Lady Zinnia, only to become captive herself. And she'd dragged Thorn along with her.

She'd found them all right! They were here in the Dark Lands, as she'd suspected. In fact, they were lying against the wall across from Ping and Thorn! But what were Lord Sycamore's plans? He wouldn't hurt his own son, would he? Possibly not, but she wasn't sure about the rest of them.

After Lord Sycamore and Lord Evergreen had carried Ping and Thorn up the stairs to this loft, they'd bound them with rope and magic and pushed them to the floor.

Sycamore tried to take Thorn with him from the

tower, but Thorn had given Sycamore a well-placed kick and said he wouldn't leave Ping. "We're a team, and teams stick together!"

"We'll see about that, Hawthorn," Sycamore had said with a scowl. "You'll be a team of one soon."

They left and the tower door below slammed shut with a loud bang. No bars imprisoned them, but the invisible magic holding them captive in this tower was strong and frightening. She could sense it all around her. Is that why her head pounded in rhythm with her heart?

Ping gazed at the slumbering figures. Lady Zinnia appeared less haughty in vulnerable sleep, and Queen Aster exhibited regal charm even in rest. They hadn't woken up when Ping and Thorn arrived. Was their sleep enchanted? The lump in Ping's throat grew as she gazed upon the queen. This was the woman she had dreamed about since discovering her own identity. The woman she'd admired in the royal painting. The woman who had sent Ping away to keep her safe.

As she watched her mother's chest rise and fall and examined her face, looking for traces of herself, the realization settled in Ping's heart. This was the mother she'd wished for and wondered about all her life. She had longed for this moment, imagined it in vibrant colors, but the reality was a bundle of emotions she scarcely understood.

Was this the same whirlwind feelings Frigg had experienced when she'd found her own mother after a long absence? Frigg had discovered her own mother and brought her home to Nadavir. When she'd first seen Namis, did Frigg feel a sense of love?

That's what it felt like to Ping. A love she had always desired. A love that had kept them apart. A love that could only exist between a parent and child filled that space inside her as she watched her mother sleep.

"Well, this is a fine mess! How will we escape?" Thorn said, shaking Ping out of her thoughts. Despite their predicament, she smiled to hear a friendly voice.

"I don't have any idea how to escape," Ping mumbled, her words slurred by the magic in the air. "This enchantment is making me woozy. Can you do anything to reduce it?"

"I'm afraid my father's magic is too strong for me to overcome," Thorn confessed with a heavy sigh.

They lay back to back, so Ping couldn't see his face, but her heart ached for him, knowing he suffered a storm of disbelief at his father's betrayal.

"Oh, Thorn, your father. I'm so sorry! This must be a terrible shock."

Her friend remained silent. After a moment, he cleared his throat and spoke. "My head may explode from my thoughts about my father. His deeds are a burden too heavy for me to bear. To capture Queen Aster, Lady Zinnia, and you." In a hushed voice, he added, "and his own son."

The scurry of tiny feet interrupted them. A small voice squeaked, "Princess! And Master Hawthorn! I'll chew those ropes right off you."

"Chia, your bravery brings light to our gloom!" Ping cried with relief.

Thorn was more hesitant. "These ropes are thick.

Can one small mouse bite through?"

"I can try."

The ropes on Ping's wrists wiggled and determined nibbling noises offered a melody of hope.

CHAPTER 32

Reunited at Last

As twilight descended upon the Dark Lands, Iris returned to their hideout in the trees. She'd been checking out the tower. With a flourish, she presented a net with a handle containing two small creatures.

"Spiders?" Frigg asked, intrigued to hear Iris's explanation.

"Yes, indeed," responded a proud Iris.

"Why did you capture spiders?" Tip asked.

Cricall munched grass, swallowing to ask, "And where did you get the net?"

With a sparkle in her eye, Iris explained. "Crafted it by magic. Didn't know I could do that, but these spiders emerged from the tower. I brought them here for questioning. Anyone speak spider?"

"I do," Frigg said. "I talk to spiders in the Nadavir caves. Maybe these spiders speak the same language."

Cricall leaned in, his gaze meeting the sixteen

unblinking eyes that stared back. "Check out all those eyeballs! Wonder what they've seen."

"Free them," Tip urged.

"They'll escape," Iris said, her lips curving into a pout.

"They may not talk if they feel trapped," Tip said. "And they haven't done anything wrong."

Frigg spoke to the spiders in a soft voice, "I'm Frigg, and these are my friends. We've journeyed far to find my friend Ping, a pixie faery."

At the mention of Ping, the spiders jumped with excitement. "Yessss!" they shouted. "We know Princess Ping! She needs help!"

Frigg translated for the others. "Let them out," she said to Iris.

With care, Iris lowered the net, and the spiders scuttled out.

"Can you lead us to Ping?" Frigg asked.

"Yessss," the spiders chittered, their legs a blur as they led the way to the tiny gap in the tower.

Cricall balked at the tiny entrance. "That hole is way too small for us!"

Iris measured it with her eyes. "As a dragonfly, I can squeeze through." With a shimmer, she transformed and flitted after the spiders.

Soon, a door appeared in the wall, a lock clicked, and scraping sounds filled the air as the door opened. Iris flew out. "Standard vanishing spell. Easy to break, if you know how."

They rushed inside and surveyed the empty lobby. Cracks snaked across the walls, while cobwebs hung from the ceiling like ghostly shrouds, giving it the appearance of a forgotten relic.

Tip pointed. "Stairs!"

The air inside the tower was heavy and stagnant, making it difficult to breathe as they climbed the staircase, which seemed to stretch endlessly upwards. When they finally reached the top, they came upon a most peculiar sight. Four pixies were bound by ropes and a diligent mouse urgently gnawed the bindings.

Frigg stared at the one pixie she recognized. "Bloated Bedrock Bugs! Ping, you're alive!" Tears of joy and relief streamed down her cheeks.

Ping's mouth dropped open, and her eyes widened. "Frigg! Tip! Cricall! Iris! And a black and white fluffy creature with long ears! Welcome to my prison tower! How did you get pixie sized? Never mind, please, get me out of here!"

Once the initial shock of seeing her friends subsided, Ping eagerly introduced everyone.

Frigg said, "And this is Speckles, a new friend we met on our journey."

Speckles dipped her head and said, "I'm so glad to meet you, Princess Ping." Then, noticing Chia's diligent efforts to gnaw the ropes binding Ping and Thorn, she said, "Mouse teeth may be sharp and mighty, but rabbit teeth are larger and mightier. I'll gladly help, and together we'll have you free in no time!" With a decisive nod, she joined Chia on a rope-chewing mission.

When Ping and Thorn were free, Chia and Speckles turned their attentions to the slumbering Queen Aster and Lady Zinnia.

Frigg remembered the dagger she carried. "Your teeth and jaws must be tired." She handed Tip her dagger, and he went to work freeing the sleeping women.

Cricall offered to heal wounds left by the ropes. Ping and Thorn gratefully accepted. With a touch of his horn, his magic flowed, soothing their tender wrists and ankles. The redness faded away.

Ping rushed to Frigg and did the one thing she had longed to do all her life. She gave her a hug. A real, arms-wrapped-around-each-other hug. It felt incredible!

"It's so strange to be the same size!" Ping cried.

Frigg laughed. "Yes, we are, and I've learned so much being smaller. I can't wait to tell you about it."

Meanwhile, Tip had discovered that, although the door allowed them to enter the tower, a magical barrier prevented them from leaving. Spinet and Webwick scurried over stone and wood, their tiny legs and multiple eyes searching for hidden buttons or levers that might aid the faeries' escape.

Ping shared her tale of the last few days, filled with confusion, bravery, and hope. Her gaze lingered lovingly on Queen Aster. "This is my mother. A mysterious enchantment ensnares her and Lady Zinnia in sleep," she said, her voice quivering slightly.

Thorn picked up the story. "We found our way to this tower. When they captured us and brought us inside, we discovered Queen Aster and Lady Zinnia." He pressed his hand to his head. "I'm sorry. The magical spell trapping us in this tower also clouds our minds. We must awaken the others and escape."

"It doesn't seem that it's affecting us," Frigg said, looking to the others for confirmation.

Tip and Cricall shook their heads.

"I feel fine," Speckles said.

Iris hurried to her sister's side. "The magic is powerful. I broke through one enchantment when I opened the door below, but the magical snare preventing escape is beyond my powers. I can't see the threads weaving this sleeping enchantment." She turned to Ping. "Do you know who wove these spells?"

Thorn hung his head. "My father."

"Lord Sycamore?" Iris sighed. "I was afraid of that. His magic is powerful."

Ping rose, wings fluttering in fury. "He and Lord Evergreen captured my mother and Lady Zinnia. Sycamore's treacherous plan is to seize the throne."

Frigg, her expression laced with sympathy, said, "Oh, Ping, my heart aches for you. And Thorn, this must be shattering. Did you suspect your father's intentions?"

With a sorrowful head shake, Thorn replied, "No, I'd have tried to stop him if I'd known. I feel a fool for being deceived. My own father, such betrayal!"

Ping placed her hand on his shoulder. "He tricked us all. You've been a loyal friend to me in a land of strangers. I wouldn't have found my mother without you."

"A lot of good that did!" Thorn lamented. "Look where it got us—trapped in this tower."

Tip shook his head. "Not your fault. But all this yapping isn't getting us out of here."

Frigg agreed. "Yes, we need a plan."

"If only Queen Aster and Lady Zinnia could help with the plan," Ping said with a frown. "We must break their slumber spell."

Iris examined her sister and Lady Zinnia again, inhaling the enchanted air that held them in their sleep. "Ping, have you received your wand?"

Ping revealed her shiny wand, eliciting an awe-filled gasp from Frigg.

Iris brandished hers. "Excellent! Together, we'll amplify my magic. Hold it like this." Sparks flew from the tip, causing the others to retreat in alarm.

Ping mimicked the action, coaxing a few star sparks from her own wand.

"We'll encircle the ladies with a cascade of sparks. Gather your inner power, and when I say so, channel it through your wand. Can you do this?"

"I can try," Ping replied, her confidence wavering.

"You're saving your mother. You WILL succeed!" Iris declared, eyes ablaze and determination etched on her face.

Ping squared her shoulders and lifted her chin. "I WILL do it!"

Iris smiled. "That's the spirit of a true princess!"

Thorn ran forward, leaf wand in his hand. "I can help!" His wand brought forth golden oval sparks that resembled tiny seeds.

Ping focused on building power, envisioning sparks rising from her toes, climbing her legs, and pooling in her stomach. Heat surged as it inched up her neck and coursed down her arms. The sparks intensified, bouncing off one another. When she thought she could contain them no longer, Iris commanded, "NOW!"

Ping extended her arm, aiming her wand at the slumbering women. Iris and Thorn did the same. Silver and gold flashes burst from their wands, swirling around the two women.

Though Ping couldn't hear the incantations Iris muttered under her breath, they intensified until her aunt's voice boomed. "Awaken! Pixiandria needs you!"

Ping poured everything she had into the steady stream of sparks and concentrated on the women. Like Thorn, her arm trembled, the internal blaze intense.

At last, movement caught Ping's eye—first Queen Aster and then Lady Zinnia. They stirred, their gazes clearing.

"Ease off. Slow the sparks and cool your bodies," Iris instructed.

Ping remembered The Ancient One's teachings about calming the heat within, picturing a tranquil brook to dampen the sparks to twinkles and then mere glimmers.

Iris waved her wand, and it disappeared. "Aster, are you well?"

"I believe so," Aster responded. Suddenly, she recognized the faery before her. "Iris! You've come!"

The sisters hugged, laughing. Iris pulled back and locked eyes with Aster. "Dear sister, someone is here you should meet." She winked at Ping.

Puzzlement grew in Aster's eyes until they rested on the necklace adorning Ping's neck and recognized the beads encircling the tiny bottle. She whispered, "Can it be? My Peony?" She focused on Ping's face. With a wide grin, she opened her arms, and Ping flew into her mother's embrace.

When Ping wrapped her arms around her mother for the first time, a hug she had painted in her imagination every day of her life, her heart did a little skip and jump. It brimmed with so much joy, it could have exploded into a million sparkles. It was like being snuggled in the coziest quilt, sending love tingling from the tips of her pink curls down to her toes.

All the years she'd spent wishing and hoping melted into a golden puddle of peace, and she knew, for that moment, that everything in her life was perfect.

Lady Zinnia's voice, firm but not lacking in empathy, broke the silence. "While mother and daughter reunite, I'd like to know who you people are and what has been happening during our slumber."

After introductions and explanations, Zinnia said, "We must act with haste. Lord Sycamore and Lord Evergreen may return any moment with reinforcements to ensnare us once more."

"Reinforcements?" Frigg asked.

"Yes, as Guardian of Protection, Lord Evergreen controls the Pixiandria Guard. We don't know how many guards might be involved in their traitorous plan," Lady Zinnia explained.

Queen Aster, with a seasoned leader's grace, took charge. "Indeed, Peony and I shall have our time to share stories later." Her eyes gleaming with anticipation, she said, "We have so much to catch up on!" But suddenly, her gaze clouded over in confusion, and she slumped to the ground.

"Mother!" Ping's cry pierced the air, her wings beating in distress.

Zinnia collapsed beside her, the same muddled expression sweeping over her features. "I believe rest would be in order," she whispered.

Frigg said, "I don't think the spell is entirely gone."

Iris's forehead wrinkled. "I'm afraid you're right."

"If it pleases, Your Majesty." Cricall stepped forward, lowering his horn. "I offer a healing touch to restore your strength."

Queen Aster, her energy fading, managed a slow nod. "Yes, please."

Ping took to the air. "While they recover, let's plan."

CHAPTER 33

A Faery Triad

The group gathered in a circle. Ideas for Lord Sycamore's defeat and their escape from the tower flew as freely as the Pixiandria ravens. Before long, they had crafted a plan and set to work.

First, Spinet and Webwick sent out a silent call to their eight-legged kin. A spider army answered and set to work, spinning a dense tapestry so robust it could shield the faeries and their allies from sight. Then they created a net that covered the ceiling.

Chia escaped outside through the tiny hole in the wall, which didn't seem to be affected by the enchantment blocking the door. He planned to stand watch for the lords and rally nearby mice.

Speckles hopped down the stairs to carve a network of tunnels beneath the dirt lobby floor, a trap for anyone heavier than a spider or mouse.

Tip said with a chuckle, "You know, Speckles, the

faeries who attack will be flying, so they'll never walk on your clever trap. You'll probably only catch Cricall or me."

Speckles exhaled a soft sigh. "I hadn't considered that." Her face brightened. "I'll ask the spiders to scratch a pattern into the dirt above the tunnels. It'll be a secret map for places you should avoid."

When Queen Aster and Lady Zinnia had recovered sufficiently, they added much power and inspiration to the preparations. Lady Zinnia, wand firmly in hand, conjured a shielded barrier behind the spider's silken screen, a temporary sanctuary should their plans go awry.

Everyone surveyed their stronghold for further measures they might take.

Chia burst in, gasping for breath, with news rippling with alarm. "Lord Sycamore is coming. He's brought an army!"

"Army?" Ping whispered. Everyone exchanged nervous glances.

"My soldiers wouldn't attack me!" Queen Aster cried.

Then Chia uttered words that sent shudders through everyone. "Not soldiers. Giant creatures with curled tusks and lights attached to their snouts."

"Lights on their noses!" Iris wrung her hands. "Oh dear! The lantern creatures."

Frigg recalled, "One nearly sniffed us out, but my stinky bush confused it."

Lady Zinnia asked, "Stinky bush? That's certainly a tale for another time." She turned to Iris. "Do these beasts wield magic?"

Iris frowned. "I can't say, but their fangs are huge."

Tip and Cricall caught the tail end of the conversation. "Speckles has just the trap for them below!"

"We can hope it ensnares them." Queen Aster sighed. "If they're as big as you say, magic may be our best hope."

Queen Aster summoned her wand and, with a graceful swirl, cast a spell on the floor. Ping flitted above the now crystal-clear surface, which had transformed into a window to the lower level.

Aster assured them, "This enchanted floor is as solid as the earth itself, and those beneath us are unaware of our watchful eyes."

Frigg, doubtful, peered at the transparent surface. "I think I'll observe from over here."

"Incredible!" Thorn buzzed with excitement and zipped to Ping's side. "We'll be able to see everything that happens below."

Tip and Cricall rushed back downstairs. Tip grabbed a broom leaning against the wall. They crouched in a shadowy corner, poised to strike.

Speckles appeared unsure what a tiny rabbit like her could do to fight such enormous creatures, but she practiced delivering a few mighty kicks with her powerful back legs. Ping silently applauded her efforts from above.

The sound of the door lock clicking echoed through the tower, and Lord Sycamore soared in, his sharp eyes sweeping the lobby. Upon spotting the odd little marks on the floor, he scoffed at the harmless insect tracks.

He whistled and the lantern-nosed creatures charged in, only to tumble into the trenches created by their feet caving in tunnels. Their squeals echoed through the tower as the collapsing soil trapped them.

Lord Sycamore stared in disbelief, but remained airborne, away from whatever danger ensnared his creatures.

Spiders and mice scurried forward, biting the creatures who tried to throw them off. But the teeth on the tiny attackers were sharp and once they'd bit through the tough hides, they fiercely held on!

Tip and Cricall charged from their hiding place. Tip brandished the broom, and Cricall fought with his hooves and horn. They batted, stomped, and poked at the creatures whose squeals grew louder.

When Lady Zinnia witnessed Lord Sycamore raising his hand to summon his wand, she beat him to the spell, casting a freezing enchantment his way. He hung in mid-air over the staircase, unable to move. Still weakened from her imprisonment, Zinnia grimaced in the pain of holding the magic. Aster flew forward and added her power to the spell. Together, they confined Sycamore in a suspended flight.

Meanwhile, Tip and Cricall fought on. A creature swung his head, and the point of his tusk grazed Tip's leg. The elf screamed and swayed, but righted himself before he could topple into a burrow. He rubbed his leg and shouted a warning. "Watch out for their tusks!"

"Yikes!" Cricall cried out and leaped away, narrowly avoiding being impaled by another creature's tusks.

Tip said, "Let's try to force them out the door!"

Cricall nodded. He shoved his horn under one creature's belly and tried to lift it, but it was too heavy. Frustrated, he poked its hind end. It jumped straight up and then onto the smoother, solid surface. Cricall's second poke sent it running through the open door.

Tip grinned and jabbed another creature on its bottom with the broom handle. One after another, the creatures stampeded toward the door, sometimes falling into another trench, but urged by the pokes of Tip and Cricall, all the creatures escaped.

Upstairs, Ping could see from the sweat on her mother's brow and Zinnia's trembling wand arm that they could no longer hold Sycamore frozen on the staircase.

Aster shouted, "Everyone ready for phase two!" Ping, Frigg, and Thorn rushed to their assigned positions. She and Zinnia lowered their wands and released the spell on Lord Sycamore.

Ping, hair white with terror, huddled with the others as her mother slipped behind their magical barrier. The eerie squealing of the lantern-nosed creatures still echoed in her mind and sent chills up her spine. Hovering beside her, Queen Aster wrapped a comforting arm around her shoulders. With a gentle squeeze, she whispered words of courage into her daughter's ear.

Ping rekindled her resolve, turning her hair an invincible blue. Lord Sycamore had deceived and kidnapped her, but now it was her turn to defeat him. She wouldn't crumble. She, Princess Peony of Pixandria, encircled by her mother's love and the steadfast support of her friends, would rise to her royal calling. Any thoughts of falling apart would have to wait.

They braced for Lord Sycamore's entrance, a tense silence enveloping them.

A fireworks explosion and a resounding BOOM shattered the stillness and their meticulous plans as Lord Sycamore burst into the loft chamber. The magical ceiling net meant to trap him fizzled away, and the webbed silken screen splintered, sending the figures hidden behind it sprawling.

Lord Sycamore stood amidst the chaos, surveying the scene with bodies crumpled on the floor. There was no joy in his eyes when his gaze landed on his own son, silent and unmoving. As he drew closer, the figures flickered and vanished like a mirage, leaving him looking bewildered.

A melodic chime from the other side of the chamber halted him, and he turned to witness an enormous translucent bubble materializing. Inside it, the faeries he thought vanquished hovered, defiant and unbroken.

A dark and foreboding laugh clawed its way from Lord Sycamore's chest, a sound that was both a growl and a roar, filled with malevolence.

Queen Aster challenged him with a scowl, her voice filled with righteous anger. "How dare you threaten the crown!"

"Do you, with no blood claim to the throne, honestly believe you can best me?" Sycamore sneered.

"I rule this realm by the laws of Pixiandria, and I will not relinquish that leadership to a traitor like you."

"You cower inside your bubble claiming victory with magic trickery?"

Lady Zinnia's voice rang out behind him, filling the loft with clarity and light. "Galewing Windwhisper, I speak your true name, and with the power of that knowledge, I command you to silence."

Lord Sycamore's eyes grew wide and round. "NO! How can..." he bellowed, but his voice faltered into silence.

"I've known your true name since childhood, but never needed to claim it until now." Zinnia glared at him. "You betrayed us, so I use that knowledge to stop you."

"What's happening?" Frigg whispered to Thorn.

With tears running down his cheeks, Thorn replied so all could hear, "To know a faery's true name is to wield control over them. Lady Zinnia had that knowledge, and now we do as well. He is powerless."

Three figures soared through the barrier, their wands at the ready. As they circled Lord Sycamore, a flick of their wrists released the power that had been building inside them, weaving a tapestry of sparks that swirled around him and bound him in place.

Queen Aster spoke, "We are a triad of faery kin—queen, sister, and daughter—the strongest magic bond in all the realm. We unite our family's magic to decree your fate. I, Queen Aster, rightful ruler of Pixiandria, revoke your royal title and sentence you, Galewing Windwhisper, to imprisonment for treachery against faeries, for betrayal of the Crown, and for treason against Pixiandria."

Galewing Windwhisper, once known as Lord Sycamore, was wrapped in sturdy iron chains as the triad's spell strengthened. When he was fully restrained, Queen Aster said, "Release." She held the spell, while Iris and Ping allowed the heat of their magic to ebb away. Only then did the Queen relax her spell, leaving Sycamore ensnared, his expression etched with defiance.

Lady Zinnia lowered the barrier protecting the others and flew to embrace Thorn, who stood immobilized, gazing at his father with sorrow and resignation. "I know this weighs heavy on your heart, Hawthorn, but your courage shines above your father's deeds. We are always here for you."

And with a slow nod, Thorn accepted their support.

CHAPTER 34

Return to Pixiandria

The somber and fatigued group of family and friends trudged through the mystical portal to Pixiandria. Queen Aster and Lady Zinnia magically transported Galewing Windwhisper to a dungeon cell.

Without knowing which members of the palace guard and Kaboodle remained loyal to the queen, Zinnia had sent Thorn ahead to contact her personal guard captain. He was waiting for them in the dungeon with a unit of trusted sentries. They had already captured Lord Evergreen, Galewing's accomplice, and were holding him in a cell nearby.

Aster and Zinnia cast an enchantment on the palace that caused any disloyal pixie to fall into a deep sleep until captured.

Everyone agreed to meet for Moonlight Morsels in the ballroom after they'd rested.

Thorn turned to Ping. "I'm going to seek The

Ancient One for help to untangle my thoughts."

"I can't imagine what you're feeling, but I'm here if you need to talk." Ping embraced him, ignoring the prickly leaves in his hair.

With a grateful nod, Thorn spread his wings and darted through the hallway. Ping watched him, her heart breaking.

As Ping led her friends through the palace hallways, she rejoiced in their expressions of awe and wonder, remembering how she had experienced the same amazement at seeing all this splendor for the first time.

Frigg's mouth dropped open when she saw the wooden column loaded with vast faery knowledge. Ping pulled a book from the wooden column and giggled at the gasps as the library produced a copy to take its place.

"Everything is so elegant!" Tip said, delight in his voice. "Why are tiny chairs and tables in those holes near the ceiling?"

Ping flew to Tip and flicked him on the shoulder. "Because pixies fly!" She soared to an alcove in the wall and plopped herself on a chair, waving to her friends below. "And we have magic!" she shouted, her laughter filling the gallery. The surrounding air sparkled, and flowers bloomed on the vines curled around the pillars.

Speckles giggled. "Wish I had some wings and magic!"

"Don't we all," Frigg said, eyes wide with joy for her friend.

"We'd never have fit in this palace if those faery crystals on the bridge hadn't shrunk us!" Cricall noted.

Ping's hair flared orange with excitement, and she swirled down to Cricall. "That's how you got small? Crystals!" She danced an air jig. "I love it so much that you're finally pocket-sized like me!"

"We do, too, but I sure hope we can get big again before we return to Nadavir," Frigg grumbled.

Speckles nodded at the library column. "There must be a growing spell to get us big again somewhere inside all this faery wisdom!"

Ping turned her hair a self-assured blue. "My mother or The Ancient One will know."

"Who's this Ancient One?" Frigg asked.

"Think Hilla, only younger and less scary."

Ping guided her friends to her chamber, where Violetta greeted them with several other attendants who showed Tip, Cricall, and Speckles to nearby cozy quarters. Ping insisted Frigg stay with her. "We've been apart too long!"

Frigg surveyed the luxurious room and agreed with wide eyes. "Quivering quarries! So much to talk about!" Her gaze landed on the massive closet jam-packed with beautiful dresses. "Let's start with the wardrobe."

After a tour of Ping's chamber, they shared pastries and tea at the table by the window. Frigg admired the beautiful gardens as they talked.

"Tell me more about this name thing," Frigg said. "You're Ping to us, but your mother named you Peony. Is that your true name? Can we control you because we know it?"

Ping giggled. "You'll never control me! Our common

flower and tree names are not our true names. They're like nicknames."

"Then how do you get true names?"

"The Ancient One told me that our parents whisper our true names in our ear when we are born. I don't remember mine, but it's in here somewhere." Ping pointed to her head. "Guess I'll have to ask my mother."

Ping flung open the window and placed a honeyed pastry on the sill and another in the corner. Soon the chamber echoed with mirth, trills, and squeaks as Frigg poured the rosehip tea, and Ping regaled her flying and crawling friends with their exploits in the Dark Lands.

"What's all this fuss?" Tip called from the doorway.

Ping invited Tip and Cricall to join the festivities. Iris floated into the chamber, close behind the others.

"My, my, my," Chia said from atop a cushion on the bed. "What magnificent merriment."

Iris chimed in, "I approve. The situation calls for a party."

Ping's smile faded. "But it's hard to be happy when my heart aches for Thorn. He's been a brave friend and now faces so much sorrow."

"He received a shock and lost a father," Iris agreed with a furrowed brow. "I'll check on him." With that, she darted from the chamber.

A timid voice piped up from the entryway. "Is it okay if I come in?"

"Speckles!" Ping cried. "Please join us. You are always welcome."

The bunny hopped into the chamber, joining the mice and spiders at the feast. Chia offered her a scrumptious carrot from the harvest platter.

When Violetta returned with a fresh bounty of treats, she hesitated, but then accepted Ping's warm invitation to join them. "I'd love for you to meet my friends," Ping said.

With the chamber brimming in laughter, Ping winked at Frigg from across the room and slipped out the door. She made her way to her mother's chamber and found Daffodil outside the door, a tea tray full of crystalline cakes floating behind her.

"Oh, Princess Peony, I mean Ping, what a relief to see you unharmed! Your absence sent ripples of worry through us."

"I regret any distress I caused you, but I'm happy we found the Queen. Thank you for the beaded bracelet. You were right—it led my mother to recognize me as her Peony."

Daffodil's laugh tinkled. "I'm glad I could help. Come, share tea with the Queen."

"Yes, I'd love that." Ping's locks turned a soft pink with delight.

Daffodil's eyes widened. "Dancing daisies! What magic have you woven into your hair?"

Ping giggled and changed her curls to a happy orange as she thought she must get Daffodil and Frigg together to compare their unique sayings. "Just a little magic I've nurtured."

"Well, it will definitely enchant your mother!"

With a twirl and heartfelt chuckle, Daffodil escorted

Ping into Queen Aster's chamber.

Mother and daughter spent several precious hours sharing tales of their lives. Ping described her life in Nadavir and learned about her father, King Rowan. Her mother expressed regret for sending her away. "It was the only way to keep you safe."

"But why didn't you send Iris for me sooner?" Ping asked.

"The danger persisted, and the risk to you remained."

"And now? Is the danger passed?"

"I can't say with surety, but I just received word from Lord Beech, the new Guardian of Protection, that the guards found dried aparbite root hidden in Galewing's home. The plant is banned in Pixiandria because it's so toxic." She paused and took a deep breath. "It's the poison that was suspected in Rowan's death. We can't be sure unless Galewing confesses, but there is a strong possibility that he killed your father."

Ping's hand flew to her mouth, and her eyes opened wide. Her mother gathered Ping in her arms. "It answers a lot of questions and takes the blame for Rowan's death off me."

"I'm glad you can finally feel safe," Ping said. "Someday, I want you to tell me all about my father."

Her mother squeezed her tightly, much to Ping's delight, and then looked thoughtful. "Yes, we will have long talks about your father."

"I'd like that very much."

Aster smiled. "Zinnia and I talked truthfully when we could stay awake in the tower. We came to an understanding. Zinnia has mellowed over the years, and she greatly admires your boldness. So much like your father." A chuckle escaped her lips. "She found your courage at the Kaboodle meeting astounding. I have to say I'm rather impressed with you myself! The dwarves raised you admirably. Even better than Iris reported over the years."

Ping's hair blushed purple with embarrassment at the praise.

Queen Aster gasped in wonder. "Such a gift you possess! I've never seen the like."

"The Ancient One believes my magic blossomed to craft abilities for survival in Nadavir. It's probably why I can speak to mice, spiders, and birds."

"I can't wait to see what else you can do, my dear Peony."

A frown creased Ping's brow. "Yet I cannot sprout peonies in my hair, as other pixies do with their name flowers or trees."

"Perhaps that day will dawn," Aster said, her voice tender.

Ping hesitated, inhaling deeply. "I know you named me Peony, but everyone in Nadavir calls me Ping. I don't know who Peony is yet."

"Then Ping you shall remain! Comfort is the cornerstone of home. But do you mind if we call you Peony on royal ceremony occasions? I think it will help the pixies of the realm to accept you."

"Oh, yes! It might help me accept my Peony self, too." Ping sighed, relief filling her heart. "What should I call you?"

Queen Aster touched her cheek in thought. "In my dreams, I always heard you call me Mam. That's what faeries call their mothers. Would that be something you could do?"

Ping's eyes sparkled. "Mam, yes!" She leaped into her mother's arms.

With that hug, a new chapter to their story began.

CHAPTER 35

Where Everyone Belongs

Two weeks after the daring rescue, Queen Aster and Princess Peony perched on their thrones, which floated beneath a magnificent woven tapestry adorned with the royal crest. Seven Kaboodle members sat to the side, while two empty chairs served as a silent reminder of the traitorous lords who once occupied them.

Bursting with pride and apprehension, Ping noted the splendor of her surroundings. This was her first official ceremony as a princess, yet it wasn't a joyful one.

A hush fell over the pixies in the audience as the palace soldiers flew the first prisoner through the enormous entryway. They dropped Galewing Windwhisper into the prisoner cage in the middle of the hall. Hedgespot Stormshaper, the former Lord Evergreen, was placed in another cage nearby.

Chia's critter spies had sniffed out Hedgespot as the mysterious intruder who'd tried to kidnap Ping from her chamber.

Galewing's eyes glared defiantly at the Queen, but Hedgespot's head drooped, eyes closed in shame. Ping's heart pounded as her anger surged when Galewing's disrespect became apparent. How dare he show contempt for the Queen after the horrible things he'd done? Was his previous friendly charm just an act? She couldn't help but wonder what had driven these lords to such treachery. They'd probably never know.

A procession of conspiracy accomplices entered, surrounded by guards and arranged in several rows behind their disgraced leaders. Gasps from the crowd mirrored Ping's own shock at the sheer number of pixies involved in the attempt to overthrow the Queen. Profound sadness for her people replaced her initial shock, realizing that shattered trust had greatly wounded the realm.

Workers had built more iron cells in the dungeons to hold all the conspirators. There was no doubt the criminals would suffer long prison sentences.

Ping gazed over the crowd and spotted Thorn sitting with Frigg, Tip, Cricall, and Speckles. Their compassion for this boy, who'd been shaken by his father's treachery, had led them to befriend and support him.

Ping knew that his faery friends had deserted him, unable to separate him from his betrayer father. Ping remembered those boys laughing and chasing the zigzagging ball through a field. Birch, Catalpa, Aspen, and Willow had grown up with Thorn. She resolved to have a talk with them. Words from a princess might persuade them to reconsider their harsh feelings toward him.

A loud chime sounded. The royal herald unrolled a giant scroll and read the proclamation. As expected, all conspirators received imprisonment. Queen Aster proclaimed the sentences a royal decree, and the prisoners were flown from the hall.

Queen Aster said, "Pixiandria will require time to recover from this tragedy."

Heads nodded throughout the hall.

"The criminals sentenced today were solely responsible for their own actions. They had two leaders. However, each prisoner decided to follow them and is now paying the price."

Heads continued to nod agreement.

"I declare that the criminals' families should not be blamed or penalized for the deeds of their kin. We will embrace them into our lives and homes without prejudice."

Those who had been nodding moments before now whispered their confusion. Many in the crowd appeared to prefer grumbling over agreeing, but they shrugged their shoulders and nodded their heads once again.

Queen Aster beamed. "Wonderful!" She snapped her fingers, and a table materialized before her with shiny objects glittering in glass cases.

"Pixies are known throughout the world for spreading mischief. But we are also famous for joyful celebrations.

Before we begin our festivities, it is my immense privilege to bestow honors on some extremely worthy individuals."

The pixies, eager for a celebration, looked less enthusiastic about listening to honors being passed out to those other than themselves. But realizing there would be no festivities without honors, they applauded vigorously and hoped Queen Aster talked fast.

"Lady Zinnia, Master Hawthorn, and Lady Iris, please fly forward."

Zinnia rose from her place among the Kaboodle members and joined Thorn and Iris, who had flown to hover before the queen.

"Lady Zinnia discovered the former Lord Sycamore had kidnapped me, and she was imprisoned as well. Her intelligence and bravery helped to capture the lords responsible for the rebellion. I appoint Lady Zinnia to the position of Lady Chancellor of Pixiandria. She will act as my second in command and assist me in preparing Princess Peony to ascend the throne in the future."

Ping forced a smile, determined to discuss her reluctance about a future as a queen with her mother soon.

Thorn, looking confused and a bit frightened, was next.

Queen Aster smiled at him. "Master Hawthorn, in recognition of your courage in braving the Dark Lands to rescue your Queen, I also convey upon you the title of Lord Hawthorn, granting you the lands and properties formerly held by Lord Sycamore."

Thorn's eyes widened. His wings transformed, becoming a vibrant blend of colors that mirrored his newfound hope and strength. He bowed, tipping his wings to the Queen. The crowd, silent at first, clapped with new respect for the young lord.

"Lady Iris, my dear sister, you have performed a brave and noble service to our realm in keeping Princess Peony safe over the years. You also took part in my rescue and in the defeat of our enemies. I appoint you young Lord Hawthorn's guardian until he becomes an adult."

"I am proud to award each of you the Medal of Distinguished Service to the Crown."

As she placed the medals around their necks and kissed each of them on the cheek, the crowd applauded and cheered.

Queen Aster turned to Ping. "Princess Peony, will you please fly forward?"

Ping rose, her hair glowing lavender to the oohs of the crowd. She hovered beside her mother, unsure what was about to happen.

"I proudly present my daughter, Peony, Princess of Pixiandria. Although she has been absent from the realm at my directive, she has returned to embrace her homeland and take her place as your future queen."

The crowd erupted in wild cheers! Pixies soared and looped, their voices a jubilant chant celebrating their princess. Ping's heart pounded. The overwhelming support from the pixies was heartwarming. Did she belong to Pixiandria now? What about her place in Nadavir? As she gazed at the pixies cheering for her and turned to see the joy on her mother's face, she bit her lip and forced down the heaviness in her chest. She tipped her wings to her mother.

Queen Aster beamed with pride as she presented Ping with the Medal of Distinguished Service to the Crown.

"It is unusual for Pixiandria to welcome visitors to our land. In fact, until now, it has been unheard of. Would the noble ambassadors from Nadavir and their companion step forward?" Frigg, Tip, Cricall, and Speckles moved to stand before the Queen. It was clear from their expressions that they were bursting with awe and pride.

Gratitude and admiration for her friends flooded Ping. Their actions had been invaluable in defeating Lord Sycamore. She was proud to see them recognized.

"You have shown bravery and integrity in making your way to Pixiandria to support Princess Peony, assisting in our rescue, and in participating in our enemies' defeat. To each of you, I award special medals for your roles as Courageous Champions of Pixiandria." The friends stared in wonder as they bowed, and she placed shiny gold medals around their necks.

Queen Aster called Chia forward. He, too, was awarded a tiny medal and given gold star stickers for his spider and mice associates to wear so pixies would give them respect (and not squish them!) "I bestow upon you the title Sir Chia, Royal Palace Scout."

Chia, wiggling his whiskers with dignity and pride, brought a smile to Ping's face, and she winked at him.

The crowd was growing restless at so much medal

giving and appeared to have lost all hope of getting to the festivities. But Queen Aster's next announcement relieved the anticipation. "Let the celebration begin!"

Whoops and cheers erupted. Attendants swooped in, carrying trays heaping with food and beverages for the party that lasted long into the night. The sound of laughter and music filled the hall, intermingling with the joyous rustle of wings and the melodic chirping of birds perched on the grand chandeliers.

The next morning, Ping gathered with her friends in the raven tower to bid them goodbye. "I wish you could stay longer," she said.

"I wish so, too. But Da, Ma, and Birgit will be worried," Frigg replied. "We sent messages by dove, so they know we're safe."

Cricall wrinkled his nose. "Yeah, but Tip and I probably should have told our families we were leaving."

Tip laughed. "I'll bet Dvalin told them, and they won't be mad for long when we tell them about our adventures!"

"And share the tiny pixie crystals Iris gave us!" Frigg added.

"I'm not sure about riding ravens to Nadavir," Cricall said, eyeing the large black birds warily.

"You'll be fine with those remarkable safety harnesses the pixie craftworkers made for you and Speckles." Tip helped Speckles into her tiny seat belt among the feathers in front of a pixie rider.

Speckles turned to the rider. "Please hang on tight, kind sir. I'd hate to fall."

The rider smiled. "I've got you. No falling in your future, milady!"

Speckles turned to Frigg, "Are you sure I'll be welcome in Nadavir?"

"Definitely, Speckles! Anyone with digging skills like yours will be welcome in our underground caves!"

Iris fluttered among them and then climbed atop her dove. "When we arrive in Nadavir, I've got the spell to make you big again."

"Hope it works," Frigg grumbled.

"Me, too!" Tip said.

Ping hugged Tip and Cricall tightly, her embraces filled with both joy and sorrow. The riders assisted them in mounting their feathered steeds.

Frigg swallowed to fight down her tears, then she frowned with puzzlement. "Ping, why is your hair black? I don't think I've ever seen it that color."

"I think it's because I'm sad," Ping said with a sigh. "Seeing my dear friends leave. I'll miss you so much. I've never been this sad before."

Frigg said, "We'll miss you, too, but you'll be visiting in no time. You promised you'd come."

Ping nodded her head vigorously. "Yes, I will. Nadavir is rooted in my heart forever."

Frigg gave her a lingering hug, but as she pulled away, she poked at something pink in Ping's black hair. "What's this?"

Ping gave her a puzzled look and then, as the realization hit, she giggled, touching the flower bud growing amid her curls.

"It's a peony blossom!" Iris swooped in for a closer peek. "Oh, Ping, you've sprouted a hair sprig."

"Hair sprig?" Frigg asked.

Ping performed a loop-de-loop of excitement, her laughter echoing through the raven tower. "It's a pixie thing," she shouted. "It means I belong to Pixiandria."

She landed in front of Frigg, who frowned. "Does that mean you don't belong to Nadavir?"

Ping's smile faltered for a moment as she considered Frigg's question. "Not at all! It means I belong to both. I'm a girl with two amazing homes. I'm extra lucky."

As she said this, the emotions swirled inside Ping. She was truly excited about her new life in Pixiandria, but she carried a pang of sadness at the thought of leaving Nadavir's familiar comforts. The discoveries ahead, learning more about her role in Pixiandria, both thrilled and frightened her.

Her heart swelled with gratitude as she gazed at Frigg, Tip, Cricall, and Speckles. "I'll visit as often as I can," she promised, her voice steady and sincere. "And you'll always be welcome in Pixiandria."

Frigg's eyes glistened with unshed tears as she reached out and squeezed Ping's hand. "We'll hold you to that, Ping. You're more than just a princess to me. You're my sister."

Ping gazed at her friends, mounted on their ravens and doves. She waved until they were out of sight, feeling bittersweet joy and longing.

As she turned to fly back into the palace, Ping touched the peony blossom in her hair and smiled. She was ready to embrace her new life, knowing that she carried the love and memories of her friends with her, no matter where she belonged.

We hope you have enjoyed reading
Ping's Mystery in Pixiandria!

For more Nadavir adventures with Ping, Frigg, Tip, and Cricall, watch for book 3 in the Chronicles of Nadavir series—Coming Soon!

If you haven't read book 1, Frigg's Journey of Anasgar, check it out!

When trolls attack the Nadavir colony, it's up to Frigg, Ping, Tip, and Cricall to journey in search of the lost dwarf colony of Anasgar to find help to fight the trolls!

Don't forget to leave a review!

Readers are looking for their next reading adventure and will be interested in hearing what you thought of this book!

Thank you!

Nadavir Kids Club

If you want to have more fun with Frigg, Ping, Tip, and Cricall, sign up for the Nadavir Kids Club! Deb has created a set of FREE activities for kids aged 8-12 years to enjoy when you join the Nadavir Kids Club! You'll discover games, puzzles, crafts, stories and other fun activities in the Clubhouse.

Parents, grandparents, guardians, aunts, uncles, and educators will receive a FREE newsletter with a new activity every month and updates on Deb's books and events to share with the children and students in their lives.

Sign up at https://www.debcushman.com

About the Author

Deb Cushman is the author of fantasy adventure tales for children and teens. A storyteller at heart, she grew up immersed in the worlds of books and tales, and soon began to craft her own. Her short stories have been featured in children's magazines. Her debut middle-grade novel, Frigg's Journey to Anasgar, is the first book of an exciting new fantasy-adventure series Chronicles of Nadavir.

Through her work in libraries, Deb pursued her passion for stories, guiding students of all ages and aiding in the establishment of an arts school library.

Deb resides in the Pacific Northwest, where the enchanting landscapes of forests, mountains, and beaches spark her imagination for fantasy adventures. She likes to envision meeting a faery, visiting Narnia, and battling orcs in Middle Earth, without having to leave the comfort of her living room.

Acknowledgements

Please check out my acknowledgements, where I gratefully thank all of wonderfully helpful people who have assisted me in writing and publishing the Chronicles of Nadavir series! https://debcushman.com/acknowledgements

Made in the USA
Monee, IL
29 December 2024

72289474R00159